High Tide at Green Key

Book 2

by

Ben Reinhart

Acknowledgments

and Credits

To all my proofreaders who helped me create this fascinating story

Disclaimer

The names of real-life organizations that may coincide with the names of groups noted in this book are purely coincidental and are not intended to reflect any of these groups' beliefs or philosophies. Likewise, any real-life existence of groups or individuals noted in this book is not an endorsement or recognition of such groups or individuals. The scenes described in this book are completely fictitious, and do not reflect the actual places.

This book is completely fictional and is intended to be nothing more than entertainment to the reader.

This story is a work of fiction. It was written without the help of AI or any ChatGPT aids. Names, characters, businesses, places, events, locales, and incidents are either the products of the author's imagination or used in a fictitious manner. Any resemblance to actual persons, living or dead, or actual organizations or events is purely coincidental.

This book does contain gory scenes of murder and is only intended to add drama to the story.

HIGH TIDE AT GREEN KEY

For more novels by Ben Reinhart

visit

https://www.amazon.com/author/benreinhart

Published 12/01/2023

Table of Contents

Acknowledgments

Disclaimer

Table of Contents

PART I

Chapter 1 – King of the City

Chapter 2 – Two Weeks Earlier

Chapter 3 – The Groundskeeper

Chapter 4 – Danger Ahead

Chapter 5 – The Coroner's Report

Chapter 6 – A Thousand Miles Away

Chapter 7 – Together Again

Chapter 8 – Background Check

Chapter 9 – Suspicious Connection

Chapter 10 – Jack meets Chris

Chapter 11 – Taken

Chapter 12 – Full Scale Search

Chapter 13 – The Stakeout

Chapter 14 – A Ransom Request

Chapter 15 – Playing Along

Chapter 16 – Checking Out Marina's

HIGH TIDE AT GREEN KEY

Chapter 17 – Related Tags

Chapter 18 – Aripeka Visit

Chapter 19 – Crew Lake Wilderness Park

PART II

Chapter 20 – Allyson Myers Case

Chapter 21 – Nighttime Run

Chapter 22 – Bending the Rules

Chapter 23 – The Hunt Begins

Chapter 24 – The Rescue

PART III

Chapter 25 – Riley is Back Involved

Chapter 26 – Interviewing the Congressman

Chapter 27 – A Cast of Possibilities

Chapter 28 – Taking a Break

Chapter 29 – The Pieces Begin to Fall Together

Chapter 30 – Informant's Revenge

HIGH TIDE AT GREEN KEY

PART I

Chapter 1 – King of the City

All roads in Pasco County led to a disgraced doctor and alleged user of cocaine and meth. The man was so powerful that he was commonly referred to as the King of New Port Richey. He was their former mayor.

As the sun was about to rise on a warm middle of September morning, a Pasco County SWAT team was gathering outside the former mayor's beautiful waterfront home. They were in full tactical gear with heavy weaponry, and they could be seen emerging from a large, massive, armored vehicle.

The vehicle was known as a Bearcat. It was a tactical vehicle primarily used by law enforcement agencies to transport officers to and from hostile situations and to assist with the recovery and protection of civilians in harm's way during terrorist threats, hostage incidents, or encounters with large gatherings of aggressors.

I'm Jack Myers, currently working with the Pasco County Sheriff's Office. As a Pasco County Sheriff's Deputy, I, along with a five-member SWAT team, moved away from the Bearcat and crept to the front door of the former mayor's estate home. The Bearcat's blue and red lights and blaring siren pierced the serenity of the quiet residential street.

I pounded my fist on the front door of the two-story home, shouting, "Sheriff's Office! We have a search warrant! Come to the door!", I demanded.

No one answered.

I banged again—one, two, three, and four times, announcing myself. Still nothing. I tried yet again, screaming the same command, my fist drumming the door five more times. No response from inside the house.

I then stood aside as two members of the squad team took forced entry positions. One of them, cocking a shotgun, blew off the door's locks.

The other, lugging a battering ram, bashed the door in. Before entering, the SWAT team set off a flashbang device. Once inside, the SWAT team moved through the lower level of the house and cleared it of any humans.

Chris Duncan, a new Pasco County Sheriff's Deputy from Baltimore, was already upstairs when the SWAT team began to climb the stairs to the second floor. As they did, a single gunshot could be heard from the upstairs back bedroom.

I immediately skipped over every other step as I climbed the staircase and ran to the room where the shot was heard.

Upon entering the room, I gasped as I saw brain matter and blood completely engulfing the walls, floor, and bed. A lifeless body was draped across the bed.

However, I could tell that this body, missing half his head, was not the man that lived here. The deceased was an old man named Sam Tobias, who was apparently related to the former mayor.

HIGH TIDE AT GREEN KEY

Chapter 2 – Two Weeks Earlier

Riley McFarland, who has been with the Pasco County Sheriff's Office for several years, just left her morning briefing where she learned that she was being tagged to lead a special investigation into two severed body parts that were found in a Pasco County Park.

She looked forward to taking on this case as she knew if she could solve the mystery, it could lead to the position of Detective. This was a position she felt she deserved, despite her past lifestyle.

Riley was a middle-aged redhead who lived a very promiscuous life. She had been a drug user until her ex-lover, Jack Myers, helped her clean up her life. With her ex-lover gone almost a year, she worked hard and regained the respect of her fellow officers.

She was happy now that Jack Myers, the man that meant so much in her life, was out of her life. She heard that he had moved from Florida to Puerto Rico, and that he was living with a new, much younger, Puerto Rican girlfriend. Although a little jealous, she knew she was better off without Jack Myers.

Riley's new partner, Chris Duncan, was a Detective from Baltimore. He told her he transferred to the Pasco County Sheriff's Office, as part of a 90-day training program.

Chris was part of Baltimore's DEA operation and was a badass cop that dealt with hookers, pimps, and drug dealers. He was known to always carry two guns with him. One by his belly button and one in his sock. He had taken a bullet his first year with the DEA and spent almost a month recovering.

A new mayor in Baltimore was elected to clean up the corruption in their police force and that included its Drug Enforcement Bureau. Some informants were put into protective custody and given upwards of $10,000 if they snitched on bad cops. There was talk that this was going to put Chris behind bars along with a few of his friends.

Chris's appearance was overpowering. He was tall, around 6'3", rather good-looking, full of muscle, with dirty blond wavy hair and a thick goatee. Young and only in his mid-thirties, and only a dozen years out of college, he had just made detective.

He had volunteered to work with the Pasco County Sheriff's Office to bring some of their practices back to Baltimore as part of the cleanup process.

It was their first assignment together, and Chris rode shotgun as he and Riley drove out to Green Key Park, to interview the groundskeeper who discovered two body parts at the county park where he worked. His name was Sam Tobias.

The park's entrance was just over a mile west of the traffic that buzzed along U.S. 19, and behind the motels, pawn shops, hookers, and strip malls that adorned this roadway. This was the first time that Chris went out into Pasco County on assignment, and he took in everything he saw.

Green Key used to be an island, known in times long ago as Deer Key. It was originally a small mangrove island a short distance off the Gulf Shore on the border between New Port Richey and Port Richey, Florida.

In the 1930's a home was built on the island, and the owners submitted plans to subdivide the property for development. A causeway from the mainland was built, and a man-made beach was created to make the property more attractive to investors. When a storm washed away the beach, plans fell through.

Pasco County doesn't have natural beautiful beaches like Pinellas County, with places like Clearwater Beach and Saint Petersburg Beach. The coastline is more mangroves and seaweed forests.

In subsequent years, the beach area was again renourished, and a retaining wall constructed. The land eventually came under control of Pasco County, and a portion of the area was established as a county park.

It was officially called "Robert K. Rees Memorial Park", named after a county commissioner and head of the parks department. Locals still usually refer to it as "Green Key Beach".

HIGH TIDE AT GREEN KEY

It is now one of a collection of man-made beach parks in the county. The park is home to a 650-foot boardwalk that leads to an observation tower. A perfect place to watch sunsets or spot dolphins, cranes, and other sea birds. Local residents flock here on hot summer days to enjoy the water, and in the evening, for a good view of the sunset.

Two large picnic pavilions are there, along with grills, picnic tables and a playground. On weekends it is common to find a food vendor selling hot dogs at the park.

During their drive to Green Key, there was no chatter between them. Riley just focused on her planned meeting with Sam Tobias, the old groundskeeper whose dog found two severed body parts at the park where he works. One body part was an arm and the other was a severed head.

As usual, traffic in either direction on U.S. 19 was a bitch. The highway reflected the fast-paced life that existed in Port Richey and its neighbor New Port Richey. Shopping malls, traffic lights, cars, and lots of noise were a way of hectic life in this part of town. U.S. Highway 19 was just over a mile east of the Gulf-of-Mexico, and it was the main north-south route from Tallahassee to the bottom of Pinellas County.

If it weren't for the Waffle House across the street, you wouldn't know where to turn off of the highway to get to Green Key. Driving south on U.S. Highway 19 through Port Richey, you knew you were getting close to Green Key Road when you saw the Waffle House off to your left.

Directly across the street from the Waffle House was a little street with an even smaller street sign that read 'Green Key Road'. If you didn't have that landmark of the Waffle House across the street as a marker, you never would have expected that turning right would bring you to a place of calm and serenity.

Turning down this tiny street, Riley and Chris drove past some old houses, a few condos, and some beautiful two and three story homes each with beautiful views of the gulf. Continuing down this road another half mile, you began to make your way across a manmade causeway. The trip down this causeway moved away from the mainland and became an even narrower pathway with water on both sides. Green Key itself is about a mile past where the condos and homes ended, and is clearly out into the gulf.

Continuing on Green Key Road was scary as the two-way roadway was only 20-25 feet wide, with gulf waters on both sides of the road. Generally, when a storm came through, the causeway was under water.

Occasionally you would see a car or two parked along the banks of the road, half into the water, and its inhabitants usually doing some fishing or putting a kayak into the water to explore the 'Robert Crown Wilderness Area'.

You will find no signs directing you to the Robert Crown Wilderness Area. It is an area only accessible by watercraft. The Robert Crown Wilderness Area is comprised of 347 acres of protected and undeveloped land west of New Port Richey and the Gulf Harbors Sea Forest subdivision.

Owned and controlled by the Florida Department of Environmental Protection, the Robert Crown Wilderness Area consisted mostly of wetlands and has historically had more bird species observed than any other site in Pasco County. Well over 200 species of common, rare, and endangered species have been reported.

Although there are some areas of high ground, they are not accessible and there are no hiking trails. This is an area of interest only to kayakers and fisherman.

Bounded on the north by Green Key Road, on the south by the Flor-A-Mar canal, on the west by the Gulf of Mexico, and on the east by the Crown canal, it is an area almost entirely surrounded by water. At the north side of the area, there is a small preserve owned by Pasco County Environmental Lands known as the Boy-Scout-Preserve. However, there is no access available into the Robert Crown Wilderness Area from that site.

Kayakers will find that the easiest way to access the Robert Crown Wilderness Area is along Green Key Road, where there are several possible launch points. It would also be possible to launch from the beach at nearby Robert K. Rees Memorial Park on Green Key.

Driving on this narrow road felt like you were leaving planet earth and driving to another galaxy that was surrounded by water. The road was lined with Mangroves and if you looked closely enough, you could see creatures in or close to the water.

Speed bumps along the causeway helped control vehicle speed. As you approached Green Key, you felt like you just drove half-a-mile through a decompression zone and onto Paradise Island.

At the end of the road, you were greeted with a round-about that wrapped around a drainage area. This roundabout would allow you to depart from the park, back the way you came in. Along the round-about were approximately thirty parking spots, all facing the wide-open Gulf of Mexico.

A large green sign with white lettering greeted you to inform you that the hours of the park were from dawn to dusk, and that Pasco County hoped you enjoyed your visit. At the bottom of the sign, it read, please leave the park as you found it.

HIGH TIDE AT GREEN KEY

It was the end of August and sunsets usually occurred account 8:30 P.M. Riley was right on time for her meeting with Sam, which was set for around 7:30 P.M. She set that time up because it was about an hour before the sun would set and Sam would begin his park cleanup chores.

Chapter 3 – The Groundskeeper

As Riley pulled into the park on Green Key, she could see Sam Tobias standing by the sign. It was exactly 7:30 P.M.

The park itself looked old and rundown. Most of the grass was dead or dying and the sand looked like it was several years old.

The first thing you saw when entering the park was the sign with the name Robert K Rees Memorial Park. The sign was surrounded by fairly large boulders, and she wondered if that was where Sam's dog found the severed body parts.

Riley had just called Sam to let him know that she was on her way and would be there exactly as planned. Sam had his dog

Grover with him as she pulled into one of the parking spots alongside the sign.

Sitting in her car for a moment to take in the beauty of the view, Riley thought back to the days when she was a young recruit with the Pasco County Sheriff's Office. She thought back of the nights that her and Jack Myers would run off to one of the sleezy motels in Pasco County and spend hours just making love. She would also do drugs to enhance the high she was getting from cheating the system.

For a moment, she found herself just gazing out at the water. Then reality set in, and she composed herself. Riley and Chris got out of her police cruiser, and she hollered out to Sam Tobias.

"Good to meet you miss McFarland. I hope I can be of help," he said as he extended his hand to shake hers.

HIGH TIDE AT GREEN KEY

Grover could see that Riley was friendly, as he just wagged his tail. He was a Jack Russell Terrier and loved people.

Riley shook Sam Tobias's hand and said, "Good to meet you too. Sam, this is my partner Chris Duncan. He's working with me on this case," she added.

Chris extended his hand and greeted the older looking man. The dog saw that its owner was safe, and just wagged its tail.

Riley looked Sam over and was not impressed. He was fairly old, she thought. A little hunched over and probably in his seventies or eighties. He had a beard that needed grooming.

His dog looked old also. She guessed the dog was about a dozen years old. "What's the dog's name?" Riley asked.

"It's Grover," Sam responded. "He's a good old dog and helps me at the park every night. I couldn't do this job without him," he added.

"Can you take us to where your dog found the two severed body parts?" Riley asked.

"Yes Ma'am," Sam responded. "It's right over here."

Sam led the way past the restrooms and over along the shoreline where twelve to twenty inch boulders were used to help hold the sand in place. "Right in this spot," he said.

Sam said, "Grover was sniffing the area where the arm and the head were originally found last night. The body parts have been removed by your Medical Examiner earlier this morning and taken in for identification."

Riley walked up to the exact spot where the severed arm and head were found and looked around. The area hadn't been disturbed and there were on signs that anything had been moved. That seemed to rule out the thought that the body parts were placed here.

She looked around and said, "There's no blood here, so the body parts were not severed here. Have you seen any blood anywhere else in the park?" she asked.

"Nope," Sam replied. "The body parts were right here. Lodged in between these boulders," Sam said bending down and pointing to exactly where the two body parts were found.

"Now that I've had a chance to think things through," Sam continued, "I'm guessing the two body parts floated in with the tide, and that the decapitation occurred out in the gulf. Not sure what caused the decapitation though," he added. "Or who did it."

"Does the gulf have high and low tides?" Chris asked.

"Sure," Sam responded. "Just like the oceans, but not as significant. And, sometimes only once a day whereas the tide changes twice a day in the ocean. Here in the gulf, it only rises and falls less than a meter, but in the ocean it can rise and fall up to two meters."

"What exactly do you do here, and what time did Grover find the body parts?" Riley turned to Sam and asked.

"I begin cleanup of the park around 9:00 P.M., after the park is empty. The sunset occurs around 8:30 P.M. and once that happens, everyone leaves. Some leave quicker than others, but usually they're all gone by 9:00 P.M."

"What time did you notice what Grover had found?" Riley asked.

"About an hour after everyone left the park," Sam answered. "I think it was around 9:30 P.M. Maybe a little later than that," he added. "Grover is a good dog, and he helps carry some of the trash over to me that the visitors leave behind," Sam said petting the dog.

"Grover didn't touch the two body parts, but rather just stood there where he found them and barked. When I went over to see what he was barking at," Sam continued, "I saw the arm and the head. The head was staring up at me."

"I was hoping he wasn't barking at a snake or something, but when I saw what was there, I heaved my guts out. I'm too old for this kind of stuff," Sam said starting to hyperventilate. "I was afraid that these body parts were cut off here at the park, and that whoever did this was watching me find the parts. Then I thought that they would be coming back to do the same thing to me," he added.

Riley took pictures with her cellphone of the spot where the two body parts were found. She then took additional photos of the distance between the boulders and the waterline. "I'll need to pinpoint where the tide was now and last night, but that should be easy to do," she said to Chris.

"Were there a lot of people at the park last night," Riley asked.

"I'd say it was a normal night. Most of the visitors to this park are couples. They bring blankets and lay them out in the sun, or they sit on benches along the water. Last night, there were probably around thirty couples here.

"When the sun starts to set they hold hands and kiss," Sam said. "Last night was a beautiful sunset. Many of the couples were embracing as they watched the sun disappear from the sky. I've seen some even have sex on the beach. That's only when I get here early," Sam added.

Riley made note of that comment and put an asterisk next to what she wrote down. She wondered if that's how this old codger got his jolly's off.

"Did you see anyone who you thought shouldn't be here?" Riley asked. "Anything unusual? Was there anyone here that wasn't with someone else? I assume the couples that come here are regulars and that you'd recognize anyone who was out of place?" she asked.

"Nope, I didn't see anything out of the ordinary," Sam responded. "And Grover didn't act like something bad was about to happen," he added. "Like I said before, I think the body parts floated in with the high tide."

Chapter 4 – Danger Ahead

"There were a couple of fishing boats off in the distance that I saw when I arrived, but I didn't see anything floating in the water that could have made it to the shore," Sam said as he looked at his watch.

An hour had gone by, and Riley could see the sun beginning its early dissent into the water below. She thought about how lucky the couples that came here were to view earth's spectacular event. She began to envision her and Jack, sitting on a blanket on the beach, kissing and holding hands.

Stopping herself from getting emotional, she thanked Sam for his time, and his help, and made her way back to her vehicle. Chris took her cue and immediately got into her vehicle also.

Riley started up her SUV and began her drive out of Green Key on the same road she came in on. She felt as if she was leaving Paradise Island and heading back to the mad mad world of Pasco County. Something she didn't want to do.

That's how being at Green Key made everyone feel. She wanted to come back soon, and spend her time lying on the beach, daydreaming about a make-believe world where everything was beautiful. A world that Jack was in.

She caught herself weakening and having thoughts she didn't want to have. She knew that having Jack here with her would lead back to a life she had that wasn't productive. It was fun and sexy, but not in her best interests.

And the one thing she didn't want to lose again was the respect she had from her department. She was a Pasco County

Sheriff's Officer and that meant everything to her. Well, almost everything.

As Riley began driving back to the main highway along the causeway, just ahead, not even a hundred yards from the park, was a dark gray sedan that was turned sideways and blocking her path. There was a female lying in the roadway, with what appeared to be blood oozing from her head.

Riley stopped her SUV as she approached the vehicle. There were no shoulders to pull over to, so stopping in the middle of the road was her only option.

Behind the dark gray sedan that was turned sideways, was a Pursuit motorhome with the word *"Pursuit'* below the front window. The motorhome was not moving either and was obviously blocked by the dark gray sedan. It also was heading in the direction of Green Key.

There were no signs of anyone getting out of the motorhome to help the woman, so Riley said to Chris, "wait here. I'll check this out."

She exited her SUV and ran to the woman's side that was lying in the roadway. She thought about calling 911 for what appeared to be a serious accident, or phoning in that an accident was in progress, but felt the people in the motorhome should have already called for help. She also felt that the woman lying in the roadway needed immediate attention. She didn't want to delay assistance.

Bending down to assess the situation, three men came out of the motorhome and, it appeared, also came to the woman's aid. All three men had long beards and hair to match. They were young and didn't look friendly, but Riley didn't care at that moment. She knew Chris was watching her and was her backup. She also figured the woman in the roadway was more important than her own safety.

Riley carefully raised the bloody head of the woman and saw that the blood was coming from her nose. "Are you okay?" Riley asked.

"I think so," the lady said. "I just lost control of my vehicle when I carelessly let my car leave the pavement and it hit the sand on the side of the road. I was reaching for my cell phone. My nose took the brunt of the accident as it slammed into the steering wheel. I was coming to meet up with my son and his girlfriend. We were going to watch the sunset together."

One of the young men from the motorhome asked, "Should we call 911?"

Riley ignored the young man's question, "What's your name Ma'am?" Riley asked the lady lying on the ground.

"Debbie," she responded. "Debbie Johnson. I think I'm okay, and don't really want to be an embarrassment to anyone." Debbie saw my uniform and asked, "Do I need to call 911 or report any of this to the police?"

Riley explained that if her nose was the only problem, then just get back into her car and let the normal traffic flow.

The three young men that were in the motorhome agreed, as they walked around and behind Riley. The taller one bent down as if to grab Riley but noticed someone sitting in Riley's vehicle and instead, helped lift the injured woman to her feet. Chris was watching the tall man and noticed him look his way.

Within a few minutes, everything was back to normal. The three men backed up their motorhome so the injured lady could straighten out her car and continue on to Green Key.

HIGH TIDE AT GREEN KEY

Climbing back into her vehicle, Riley said to Chris, "That was easy. Ready to call it a night?" she asked.

"Yep," Chris said. Take me back to our office so I can get my car."

"Do you think we should put this into our report of the conversation with the groundskeeper?" she asked Chris.

"I wouldn't," he responded. "Just more paperwork and it has nothing to do with our visit," he added.

HIGH TIDE AT GREEN KEY

Chapter 5 – The Coroner's Report

The next morning, Riley returned to her office and was undecided about whether to file a report on the traffic incident at Green Key.

A lingering question she had was why the motorhome was driving toward Green Key. The three men never explained their journey and the question remained a mystery. Were they really just going to view the sunset? Was their intent something else.

It was 8:30 A.M. and she decided not to file a report on the traffic incident she saw. There was no one hurt and there was no need for any type of insurance claim. Rather than do two hours' worth of paperwork, she pretended that this event never happened.

Chris, who arrived twenty minutes after Riley, agreed with her decision. He logged onto an open computer and saw that the coroner had sent over a report on the two severed body parts.

The report was short and didn't say much about what was found. He opened it up and read it out loud.

The report began with a profound statement that the two body parts were not from the same person. DNA indicated that although the two body parts were from two individuals that were related, they were from different family members. However, the identities of the two men were still unknown. Dental records were in the process of being scanned. The coroner did indicate that there was a total loss of blood from the two body parts, indicating that they were not severed where they were found because there was no human blood at the scene.

The report indicated that additional information should be available shortly. There were two items under the caption of SPECIAL NOTES. The first said that the severed arm was twisted off as it was being cut. The second said the head had its eyelids glued open.

Riley was listening to Chris read the report out loud and had her head resting on his shoulder. She was like that. She then stood up and pulled out the notes she took during her conversation with the groundskeeper.

She read her notes:

- Mostly couples came to the park to watch the sunset.

- Everyone leaves between 8:30 to 9:00 P.M.

- Sam's dog, Grover, spotted the severed body parts around 9:30 P.M.

HIGH TIDE AT GREEN KEY

- The severed parts were not there yesterday.

- There was no blood where the body parts were found.

- The groundskeeper feels the body parts could have possibly floated in with the tide which was at high point just before 9:00 P.M.

- The rocks the two body parts were found at is a low point in the park and usually gets covered with water when the tide comes in.

Riley turned to Chris and said, "Not much to go on. I have a feeling we are missing something really big that happened at Green Key."

"What do you mean?" Chris asked.

"Well, I'd like to know why that motorhome was going to Green Key. Why bring a motorhome to such a small place."

Chris agreed and said those were good

questions and that we'll need to answer them.

Chris then noticed that there was a follow-up report provided by the coroner's office to the Pasco County Sheriff.

He called that to Riley's attention and read it out loud:

An identification has been made from DNA of the two body parts found on Green Key. The arm belonged to a man by the name of Aaron Russo, and the severed head belonged to David Russo. They were brothers and both men were not from Florida. There is no address on file in our state for them.

The coroner also indicated that there was a sedative in the mouth of the head, indicating that the head was probably removed after the person was dead. At least his report said that the coroner hoped that was the case.

==================

When Riley sat back down at her own computer, she noticed that her email flag was lit, indicating that she had emails that hadn't been read yet. She clicked on the email icon and her screen lit up with a dozen or so unread emails.

Quickly scanning the list, she noticed that there was an email from Jack Myers. Without hesitation, she opened the unread email and as she read it, she began to get excited.

The words she was reading made her feel like she was having a hot flash, something she was beginning to experience on a daily basis. Riley re-read the email to make sure she was reading it correctly:

> "Hope you're doing well. I just wanted to let you know that I am returning to Florida, tonight, for a short visit, to

straighten out some problems with my pension checks. I'll be renting a car at Tampa International Airport and staying at the Grand Hyatt hotel on Rocky Point until I get all this resolved. Can we have dinner this evening?

If you'd like, meet me across the street from the hotel at the Bahama Breeze around 7:00 P.M. I'll have a table out by the water."

Riley just stared at the words. She was excited that she might get to see Jack Myers again, but she was scared of what it might lead to. It had been almost a year since she'd seen him, and they didn't part on the friendliest of terms. He was chasing some young skinny girl that was young enough to be his daughter if he had one. "What was it about him that made him do that, she thought to herself."

Riley decided not to respond to Jacks email.

She figured that would give her extra time to think about whether she wanted to meet him or not.

Chapter 6 – A Thousand Miles Away

It was 10:00 A.M. and another beautiful day in Puerto Rico. When Paola left Florida a year ago, she didn't want anything to do with me. But, after a few months, she and her father needed help with finances, and she called out to me. I decided to move to Puerto Rico and keep her and her father from getting back into the drug trade. It worked for all of us.

I was sitting on the beach, sipping a Bloody Mary when Paola came bouncing out of the trailer we were living in with her father Diego Rivera. She sat down on my lap and put her arm around my neck. Then she spontaneously gave me a kiss on the cheek. "You look happy," she said.

At that moment, all I wanted to do was have sex with her. The Bloody Mary had me feeling good and she just doubled that pleasure.

"I've got to go back to the States for a few days," I told her. "There is a problem with the amount I'm receiving in my pension checks, and I need to show them what I think I should be getting, and why."

Looking sad, Paola asked, "When will you be back?"

"In a few days," I responded. "It depends how quickly I can get this resolved. Since I don't need to get a passport, I've decided to leave this afternoon. You and Diego will be fine until I get back," I assured her. "I'll leave you money for expenses, but I'll need you to drive me to Luis Munoz Marin International Airport in San Juan later today. They have a flight to Tampa International Airport at 4:00 P.M. and I'd like to be on that plane. Will that be a problem?" I asked her.

HIGH TIDE AT GREEN KEY

"No baby," she responded. "As long as you come back to me. You've grown on me, you know," she said as she kissed me again.

"I will baby," I replied. "There will never be anyone else but you," I added knowing I couldn't keep that promise. I've mellowed in the year I've been gone, but I still had my urges that needed to be dealt with. With that, I proceeded to remove Paola from my lap and head inside to pack for my trip.

At 1:30 P.M. Paola drove me to the airport, and I boarded my flight without incident a few hours later. The total flight time from San Juan, Puerto Rico to Tampa, Florida took 2 hours, 57 minutes. The drinks and the view were spectacular. As we flew over Tampa Bay, I couldn't wait to get back to my old stomping ground and see the girl I had some awesome times with.

As soon as I retrieved my luggage, I headed to the car rental facility and opted for a

Chevrolet SUV Trailblazer. I wanted to have as much room in back as I could possibly get.

I drove the ten-minute ride to the Grand Hyatt and checked in without any problems.

It was 7:30 P.M. and I was already late for my rendezvous with Riley. However as late as I was, I knew she would be waiting there for me. I wasn't wrong. There she sat with the biggest grin on her face.

She was happy to see me, and I was happy to see her.

Chapter 7 – Together Again

I pulled up to the valet parking at the Bahama Breeze and handed the keys over to a Latino dude who quickly handed me a ticket. I climbed the steps to the outside patio and there at a table by the water was Riley. She waived me over and had a giant smile on her face.

"You're late," she said removing the smile from her face.

"It took longer to check in than I thought," I told her. Just as I was about to lean over and give her a giant kiss, the waiter walked up to me and asked if I'd like something to drink.

"Please," I said. "I'll have a Ketel One martini, straight up, and stirred, not shaken."

"You look awesome," I said to Riley

meaning every word I said.

"Well, thank you," she responded. "You're not looking too bad yourself. Especially after a three-hour flight. I see you've let your white hair grow longer, and that you're wearing it in a ponytail. I also love the dark tan you've gotten while in Puerto Rico," she said.

"The flight wasn't bad after having a few drinks," I said, "and I got some much-needed rest. Seeing you here, now, made the entire trip worthwhile," I added.

"You are so kind," Riley responded. "Have you been enjoying your time in Puerto Rico?" she asked. "It looks like you've been working out. I see more muscle than when you left Florida," she added. "I hear you have a girlfriend there. Is that true?" she asked.

"Life is expensive on the big island. I'm staying with Paola and her father in a

HIGH TIDE AT GREEN KEY

trailer on the beach." I said. "It's a non-sexual relationship," I added.

"Sure," Riley said sarcastically. "Is that your choice or hers? I know you and you can't be near a woman without it being sexual," she added.

"Well, I love women," I responded. "But I'm near you and it's not sexual," I added.

"It's early yet," Riley said with a laugh. "I'm sure before the night is over, you're going to invite me up to your room for a night cap."

"Don't be so sure about that," I said. "I've got an early morning meeting with County HR people to discuss my retirement pension and it's about an hour's ride up to the government center on Little Road from here."

"So, this is all about dinner?" Riley asked.

"Yes," I said emotionally.

HIGH TIDE AT GREEN KEY

"Well, that's good to hear," Riley said, lying through her teeth.

I could tell she wanted to spend the night with me, making a lot of noise and getting sweaty. Who knows what hallway we would have ended up in.

"So, tell me, what's new?" I asked. "Are you working on anything exciting?"

"Yes," she answered hesitantly. "I'm working on an apparent double murder case. Two severed body parts were found at a Pasco County Park along the Gulf-of-Mexico. It apparently happened a couple of nights ago, and my partner and I just went to the scene where the body parts were found yesterday."

"Your partner?" I asked.

"Yes, his name is Chris Duncan, and he was just assigned to me. He's a Detective and kind of a stud, like you, but younger," she responded.

HIGH TIDE AT GREEN KEY

"Have you slept with him yet?" I asked.

"No, he's married," Riley said with a smile.

"I was married also. And that didn't stop you," I said. "So, tell me about this case you're on. What do you think happened?" I asked.

"Don't have much to tell," Riley responded. "There were no clues at the scene where the body parts were found, so I don't know much yet."

"There's always clues at a murder scene," I said. "You just need to know where and how to look for them."

"Do you want to join our team?" Riley asked. "I can certainly use your help. And this way, you'll get to meet Chris. He's a super guy. Just a little straight for me," she added.

Can you get the Sheriff to deputize me?" I asked.

HIGH TIDE AT GREEN KEY

"That shouldn't be a problem," Riley said hoping to once again be working with Jack.

Chapter 8 – Background Check

Riley had left the office early to meet up with Jack Myers in Tampa. While Riley was off galivanting with her previous boyfriend, Chris decided to take advantage of his free time and do a background check on Sam Tobias.

Chris knew from his time with the DEA that a criminal background check would reveal a person's felony or misdemeanor criminal records, any pending criminal cases, and any history of incarceration as a teenager. It is also possible to report arrests that are either pending or in progress.

He typed in Sam Tobias's name and social security number and within a few minutes, a number of PDF files were created indicating that there was information in law enforcement's database on this character.

The first PDF file provided information from almost fifty years ago, and it highlighted a series of auto thefts that Sam was involved in. Chris felt that this was good information, but rather old. Chris could tell that when Sam was in his twenties, he was mischievous, but he never killed anyone.

The second and third PDF files were more recent and indicated a more current violent past. The reports showed that Sam had a temper and that he had previously been charged with assault with a deadly weapon. However, this was over ten years ago. Still not enough to go on for a man now in his eighties.

The final PDF was very concerning and indicated that Sam was involved in dealing drugs. To be specific, he was charged with selling meth and cocaine. After a trial that included several politicians, he was convicted and sent to Marion Correctional Institution, a state prison for men in unincorporated Marion County, near Ocala.

Chris wondered why Sam wasn't in jail for these convictions. Looking deeper into the file, he saw that the then current Mayor of New Port Richey, Nicholas Tobias, rallied to his defense and had him released into a work-release program. It showed Sam was moved to Green Key Park as a groundskeeper and was allowed to serve his time working for the county. Sam Tobias was the mayor's father.

Based on the information contained in this report, Sam has been working at Green Key for two years now.

The report also showed how Sam earned extra living expenses. It indicated he would take on small maintenance jobs that involved cleaning up yards or areas that needed work.

There was a list of the employers Sam worked for and two names stood out from the others. One name was Eric Ramirez and the other was Ramone Ramirez. Both of these men were flagged as involved in other crimes. Chris knew this was very important and wanted to share this information with Riley if she ever got back.

Chris felt the connection between the groundskeeper from Green Key Park and the two individuals connected to the killings on Moon Lake was enough for a search warrant of Sam Tobias's residence. However, he decided to wait until Riley returned to review all this with her, and then request a search warrant.

Chapter 9 – Suspicious Connection

Riley returned to her office around 11:00 P.M. after having a wonderful dinner with Jack Myers.

She never did get an invite for a night cap in Jacks hotel room. She was fuming after the evening ended abruptly with Jack returning to his room alone after dinner, and not inviting her up for a night cap, but the ride back was all it took to bring her back to reality.

When she pulled up to the Sheriff's Office, she saw that Chris's car was still in the parking lot. "He's certainly a hard worker," she thought to herself. "I wonder why he's still here and not home with his wife.

"Chris," she said as she entered the building. "What are you still doing here?"

"Well, while you were out having dinner with your old boyfriend, I was here doing some research. Wait until you see what I found," he said.

"Oh, I can't wait. Do tell," Riley said in a tired voice.

"There's a connection between Sam Tobias and the Ramirez family. You remember them. They were involved in several drug related murders about a year ago. Eric Ramirez was your informant?" Chris asked.

"Sam Tobias did work for those two," he added. "Also, one important fact that I just uncovered. Nicholas Tobias, your former mayor of New Port Richey, is Sam Tobias's son.

Your mayor got his father out of prison on a work-release program and used him to distribute drugs for Ramone and Eric Ramirez."

"How did you find that out?" Riley asked.

"It's all here in police files. I just did some background checking," he responded.

She looked over Chris's shoulder again as he pointed out stuff on his computer screen. Riley saw that he was right, and that the background check showed Eric as her informant. Riley was concerned that Chris was going where he could uncover her past.

As she peered over Chris's shoulder, she could smell his cologne, even after a full day's work, and it really turned her on. She was curious how he would respond if she touched his shoulder with her chin again. "Guess there's only one way to find out," she thought to herself.

Without any hesitation, she lowered her chin until it touched Chris's shoulder. She kept it there for just a moment and then raised her chin back up. There was no response. That means he liked it and wouldn't object if she did it again.

Chris stood up, making it impossible for Riley to try the chin move again. Oh well, they'll be another time down the road.

Chris asked, "How were you able to get Eric to confess to the murder of a prostitute a year ago? Are you sure he did it?"

"I was in control of Eric," she responded. "It's not important whether he did it or not," she said. "He was my informant, and he was weak. All you men are. All I had to do was arouse him sexually and he'd do anything. I'll tell you something I've never told anyone else if you promise not to rat me out?" she said.

Leaning on Chris she whispered into his ear, "Don't tell anyone but Eric was with me most of the day when that hooker was killed, so he couldn't have killed the hooker that was left on his father's yacht. But he confessed to it, so that's all that counts," Riley said. "We closed the case and moved on."

HIGH TIDE AT GREEN KEY

Riley wanted to whisper more into Chris's ear. He smelled so good, and it really got her excited touching his ear with her lips.

"Wow, you play it rough," Chris said. "I will need to watch my back with you," he added.

"It's okay," Riley responded. "I'll watch your back for you," she added as she moved closer to Chris, but could see she was making him nervous.

"Wow, it's almost midnight. I've got to get home before my wife thinks I'm out cheating on her."

"Yea, we wouldn't want her thinking that now, would we?" Riley said as a question.

"Go, you did a good job tonight," Riley said. "I'm heading home also."

Chapter 10 – Jack meets Chris

The next morning, I was parked in front of the Pasco County Sheriff's office hoping to see Riley before everyone arrived. I was the first car there, until Riley pulled in. She was the second car there. I got out of my car as soon as she did.

"Riley!" I said in a soft caring tone. "Can we talk? I asked. "I wasn't having a problem with the amount of my pension checks. I lied. I just wanted to see you again."

I reached out for her hand and continued, "I missed you and needed a break from the pressures that I was under and beginning to find overwhelming."

"You mean overwhelming like with a woman half your age? You should know better than to go down that road. You could end up with a heart attack or a stroke," Riley responded.

"At the end of the day, I would head to the bedroom around 10:00 P.M. She just wanted to go out then. We were beginning to live two lives and they didn't intersect. I was pushing sixty and she was pushing thirty."

I paused for a moment and then said to Riley with a smile, "I'll bet you wanted to come to my hotel room last night, to get it on again?"

"Not really," Riley responded. Then hesitating, she added, "But I guess you know me better than that. "Yes, I did, and I was really pissed that you dismissed me so quickly."

"You really do love me, don't you?" I said continuing to hold her hand. "Well, I feel the same way about you. We're a pair made in heaven on the road to hell," I said.

HIGH TIDE AT GREEN KEY

As we were standing in the parking lot and laughing at each other, Chris Duncan, Riley's new partner drove up. He was the third car in the parking lot. Riley waived to him, and he came over to where we were standing.

"Jack, this is Chris Duncan, my new partner, she said introducing Jack to Chris.

I extended my hand to shake Chris's. "Nice to meet you Chris. I've heard a lot of good things about you from Riley," I responded. "Why don't we all go across the street to the Breakfast Station and have something to eat? I said.

The place was empty as it was still early. We all ordered breakfast and coffee.

"So, you're Jack Myers?" Chris said with a smile. "I pictured you differently," he added. "I can see why Riley is so fond of you. She is always talking about you," he mumbled.

"Really!" I said. "Well, it's no wonder. Last year, we cracked one of the biggest cases in Pasco County. A couple of drug dealers and a murderer out at Moon Lake. Riley got the respect she wanted from her fellow officers and deservedly so," I told Chris.

"Yes, I'm hearing all the details. Sounds like you two made a good team," Chris said.

"Well, I'm actually retired now, and just visiting Riley while back in the States. I guess you'll have to fill my shoes," I said to Chris.

"I heard about your wife," Chris said looking at Riley. "I'm really sorry," he added.

"Yes, that is a case that still needs solving. I'll probably do some checking on it while here. That is if Riley will let me use her computer," I said looking at Riley.

"No problem," she responded. "Stop bye anytime and feel free to tell me to move," she said.

"Well, how about when we finish our coffee. If I take a few minutes before your day gets started, it shouldn't be too disruptive."

We finished our breakfasts and all three of us walked across to the Sheriff's Office.

As we all walked out of the restaurant, Riley looked over to the restaurant parking lot and noticed a rather large Pursuit motorhome, parked there with its motor running.

She looked through the front window and saw two younger men, both with full beards and long hair sitting up front. There was one man standing in the doorway behind the seats. He looked like the other two men. They seemed to be staring at us.

"What a coincidence," Riley said out loud.

Chapter 11 – Taken

When we got to Riley's desk, I said, "Wow, nothing has changed. You still have your mother's photo on your desk and the clutter is still here. Your books are stacked a foot high," I continued.

"Mom's the only one I trust to not lie to me," Riley said in defense of her mess.

Riley logged onto her computer and showed Jack the coroner's report. Then she pulled out her notes from the interview with the groundskeeper and gave that to Jack to look at.

"What do you think?" she asked. "Can you solve the puzzle yet?"

"Well, it looks like the two body parts were either placed at the spot the dog found them, or they floated in during high tide.

"Good point," Chris said. "High tide was just after 9:00 P.M. Do we have any camera's showing the boats that were offshore?" he asked.

"Nope," Riley answered. "We'll have to try and get some pictures from those that were at the park that afternoon. I'll make sure the press adds that request to their story on the murders."

"Yes," I said, "let's get that request out immediately, so we can check out the boats that were there. They may have seen something or may be the culprits. Also, it's possible the groundskeeper may have taken some pictures. You'll want to check with him also," I added.

"Do you want to go out to Green Key with me?" Riley asked.

"Yes, I would," I responded. "There's got to be a few clues there somewhere," I added.

"Riley told me of the minor traffic accident

she dealt with as she was leaving the park. She explained that she came upon it as she was leaving the park from her interview with the groundskeeper,"

"What kind of minor traffic accident?" I asked.

"Well, a car heading to Green Kay was driving too close to the edge of the road, when it lost control and the car came to a stop, sideways. The driver, Debbie Johnson, hit her nose on the steering wheel and fell out the door. I stopped to see if she was okay. There was a motorhome that was behind her that couldn't pass. Both vehicles were heading to watch the sunset at Green Key.

"Okay, go ahead and call this Debbie Johnson and see if she took any pictures of the sunset, and maybe any of the boats that were just offshore that night," I told Riley.

"I didn't get the names of the three young men from the motorhome," Riley added. "I didn't think the incident had anything to do with the severed body parts."

"Tell me about the motorhome that was stuck behind the car that was turned sideways," I asked Riley. "You said there were three young men in it."

"Yes, they weren't much help, and I'm not sure why they were out there. They didn't seem the type that would go watch a sunset. It was a Coachman Pursuit, with the word 'Pursuit' on the front," Riley responded.

"Okay, this is not good. I just saw the same kind of motorhome parked across the street at the Breakfast Station. That's very coincidental," I said.

"Let me go out front and check on it. I'll pretend I'm just going to my vehicle," Riley said as she ran toward the door.

"What are you thinking?" Chris asked me. "Do you think there is any connection between the severed body parts and these vehicles?"

"No, I don't, but that doesn't mean there isn't any," I replied. "While we're waiting for Riley to return from checking out that motorhome, I'm going to use her computer to look at a recap of the Ramirez trial and the prosecutors final report. You don't mind, do you?" I asked Chris.

"Not at all," Chris responded. "I'd like to hear what you find."

It had been almost fifteen months since the murder of my wife Allyson. The case file was marked OPEN, and there were 'RELATED' tags that showed it was related to another case. The tag said 'RELATED', The Eric Ramirez case.

I didn't much care about the details of the Eric Ramirez case, so I just scanned the documents from the Allyson Myers case.

The report began with a summary that read Allyson Myers was murdered at Moon Lake Park at the beginning of the summer of last year. The report said she was clubbed to death by a large object such as a baseball bat or a four-by-four chunk of wood. The report continued by saying that drugs appeared to be involved as Fentanyl pills were found around the body.

I read about the condition of her body, and that's when the report mentioned my name as the husband, and a possible suspect. Other suspects were noted and were homeless inhabitants of the park. Several homeless inhabitants of the park were interviewed, and one said they believed the murderer was a female.

The coroner's report indicated the blows to the head were made in an upward swing, like that from a kid or a woman, rather than in a downward swing like that from a grown man.

"Not much here," I said to Chris as he peered over my shoulder as I was reading the open case on my wife.

Chris leaned into me and told me what he had just learned about Sam Tobias and that he and Riley planned to get a warrant to search the groundskeeper's home.

"Jack," Chris said. "I don't know if you're aware of this or not, but Eric was with Riley the day that hooker was killed."

"What! Where did you hear that," I responded.

"Riley told me that she got him to confess, even though he couldn't have been the murderer," Chris replied.

HIGH TIDE AT GREEN KEY

Chapter 12 – Full Scale Search

I turned around to look Chris in the face and said, "Where the hell is Riley?" I shouted. "She said she was going out to her vehicle to take a peek at the motorhome that was parked across the street. That was fifteen minutes ago," I added.

"I'll go check," Chris said as he quickly got up and walked to the front door. He was gone only a few seconds when he came running in and said, "Somethings not right. Riley was not out there, and her cell phone was lying on the ground under her vehicle. I have a feeling she has either taken off somewhere or she's been kidnapped," he said.

Those that had worked with Riley speculated that she just took off on her own and would return sooner or later. Others that knew her well said she'd never leave her cell phone behind. Maybe she just dropped it and didn't realize what happened.

Every possible officer was involved in the search for Riley McFarland. Every inch of the parking lot where Riley was last seen was searched for clues.

One older couple that was just leaving the restaurant, saw all the police commotion across the street, and came over and told us that they saw a motorhome drive across the street to the parking lot of the Sheriff's Office and they saw a female officer talking to three men alongside the giant vehicle.

The couple told us they saw the female officer get into the motorhome and then it drove away. It didn't look like the three men forced her into their vehicle.

I asked the couple, "Which way did they go once they got onto Little Road?"

"They headed that way, pointing toward the north," they responded. "And they seemed to be driving pretty fast for a large motorhome," they added.

Except for her cell phone, there was nothing providing any clues to where she had disappeared too and why. Since her cell phone was found on the pavement under her vehicle, a conclusion was made that this was a kidnapping of a law enforcement officer.

A full All-Points-Bulletin was issued for the motorhome and the three men who were inside the motorhome.

Sheriff Nocco, who came out after hearing what happened, said he would rally every law enforcement bureau within 100 miles of Tampa and hunt for his deputy.

"Come on Jack," Chris said. "Get in. Let's drive around. They couldn't have gotten too far."

HIGH TIDE AT GREEN KEY

"Right," I responded. "They've got to be within a few miles radius."

Chris yelled to the other officers, "Let us know if anything comes in on the All-Points-Bulletin that was issued. We'll be driving around as much of Pasco County as we can."

Chris burned tire rubber as he sped out of the parking lot and out onto Little Road. He showed signs that he was not happy that someone kidnapped his partner. He figured if they drove around Pasco County, and didn't see anything, that the motorhome may have left the county. I didn't agree with that thinking, but I've been gone for over a year, so maybe things have changed.

We drove north toward Ridge Road, hoping that whoever took Riley also went that way. I looked up and down every street, hoping to see a large motorhome parked in someone's driveway.

The entire Pasco County Sheriff's Office was looking for Riley.

Once we arrived at Ridge Road, we then turned east. I again checked every street and every gas station looking for a large motorhome. As we passed Moon Lake Road, I told Chris to turn onto that road and take it to State Road 52, but he ignored my request.

We got onto the Veteran's Expressway and headed south to State Road 54 and then turned west. Once back on U.S. Highway 19, we drove down through New Port Richey, hoping to spot the motorhome parked in someone's driveway. We saw nothing and no calls came in on the all-points bulletin.

Chris drove back to the Sheriff's Office, and he and I went in to talk with the Sheriff. "Any leads yet?" he asked."

HIGH TIDE AT GREEN KEY

Chapter 13 – The Stakeout

Based on the background check on Sam Tobias, Chris and I decided to stakeout the home of Sam's son, to see if they were still working together.

Chris took his personal vehicle, an old Chevy Camero, and parked it at the end of the block. I took my rented Chevrolet SUV trailblazer and sat in the back seat pretending to be drinking a bottle of whiskey.

We hoped we would see something the first night and we weren't wrong. Sam Tobias's old beat up 2001 Ford Mustang pulled into the former mayor's driveway around midnight. After getting out of his car and looking around, he went into his son's house.

I texted Chris: "Looks like father and son

are still talking to each other." Wonder what this visit is all about."

Not ten minutes later, a Coachman Pursuit motorhome pulled up and parked in front of the former mayor's home. "Holy Shit!" I said. "Do you see what I see?" I texted Chris. "I wonder if Riley is in there. It could be the motorhome that took her."

Since those in the motorhome didn't know Chris's face, he got out of his Camero and pretended to be a drunk bum as he walked past the motorhome and quickly took a picture with his cell phone of the rear of the vehicle, capturing the license plate information.

While waiting for a response, I texted Chris, who had gotten back into his car, "Do you want to check out the motorhome now, for any signs of Riley, or should we wait until we see who owns the vehicle and we get our search warrant?"

HIGH TIDE AT GREEN KEY

"Let's just check the license plate number so we can trace who it belongs to. We can't be breaking into every motorhome we see," Chris said.

"I disagree. Let's call for backup and once they arrive, we'll force our way into the house. Then you can check out the motorhome to see if she's in there," I said in a parent-child tone.

We are local Sheriff's deputies, and we don't have that kind of liberty. I was with the Federal DEA, and I learned to follow proper protocol."

"Well, I'm not going to just sit here when Riley McFarland may be inside that motorhome. I texted Chris in all caps, "BACK ME UP. I'M GOING IN".

I got out of the car and walked up to the front door of the motorhome. Pretending to be an upset neighbor, I pounded on the door until someone inside opened it up.

"You can't park here," I said. "This is my home," pointing to the house next door to the former mayor's home, "and I'm tired of large vehicles like this blocking my driveway. I can't easily get in or out," I yelled.

The driver seemed confused, and said, "Okay, calm down, I'll move it forward to the next property. That should give you plenty of room," he added.

As he was preparing to move the motorhome, I quickly scanned the inside of the vehicle, but saw no signs of Riley or any struggle she might have given. The motorhome appeared empty, and there were no signs of blood anywhere.

"Thanks," I said as I backed out of the doorway. "I appreciate it," I added.

Chapter 14 – A Ransom Request

Chris heard back on his request for the owner of the motorhome and walked up the block to meet me. He told me the Motorhome was registered to Sam Tobias.

"Well, we know the driver was a younger man with long hair and a long beard," I said. "He looked like he belonged to a domestic terrorist organization hoping to take over the country."

So, how could Sam Tobias afford a hundred-thousand-dollar motorhome? And, why would he even have one?" Chris asked. He lived down by Green Key in a run-down mobile home park. Too many questions with no answers.

"I wonder what's going on at the former mayor's home that all these people have congregated here," Chris said. "It's not Thanksgiving yet."

Confused, with no search warrant, we called it a night and went home.

When I walked into Chris and Riley's office, it was around 9:00 A.M., I saw Chris was sitting at his computer. "What did you find?" I asked. "Any updates on Riley?" I asked.

"None. She's disappeared into the wind. I think if we can answer some of the questions about this motorhome, we'll find Riley," Chris answered.

A few minutes later, my cellphone rang, and a video message appeared. The video showed Riley sitting in a chair, bound, and gagged.

The voice at the other end was distorted and said only a few words. "If you want her back, alive, we want one-hundred-thousand-dollars placed on the viewing tower at Green Key at exactly 5:00 P.M. tonight or she will die, and all you'll get back is her head." Then my cellphone screen went black.

"Holy Shit," I said. "What was that?"

"A ransom request from her kidnappers," Chris said. "At least we know she's still alive," he added.

"Not necessarily," I said. "This could have been recorded earlier. Where are we supposed to get one-hundred-thousand-dollars?

"They're playing a game with us. They want us scurrying around trying to get the money, instead of hunting them down," I said to Chris.

I quickly wrote down the details of the phone call from Riley's kidnappers and brought the information to Sheriff Nocco.

Sheriff Nocco has been in his current

position since former Florida Governor Rick Scott appointed him in 2011. He was elected to the position in 2012, re-elected without opposition in 2016 and re-elected, again without opposition, in 2020.

We were told they would pull money from our DEA evidence locker and mark it with green dye. Then he'd arrange for someone to take it out to the viewing tower at Green Key at precisely 5:00 tonight. We'll track whoever picks up the money with drones he told us.

With that part under control, I turned to Chris Duncan and said, "I think the answer is at Green Key, and I think that Sam Tobias is involved. Let's head out there early, while he's not there and see what we can see."

Chris Duncan logged off his computer and grabbed his cellphone. "Let's go," he said. "I'll drive."

The traffic was still at a peak on Little Road, as we put on our flashing lights and moved everyone over to the side of the road. Turning south toward Green Key Road, we were bumper to bumper. Our siren and lights didn't help us much. Finally, we were at the turnoff across from the Waffle House.

The Park was empty except for a middle-aged lady who was lying in the water on a lawn chair, and an old man who was watching her from a bench.

There was one car in the parking lot and a bicycle leaning against the signpost. We parked and headed toward the boardwalk that took us out to the viewing tower.

Climbing the steps to the top, I said to Chris, "We're not going to easily observe who comes to pick up the money. Maybe from drones," I said, "as they can fly upwards of 500 feet in the air.

The top of the viewing tower exposed a beautiful view of the gulf and the park itself. It was breath taking but we were not here to enjoy the view.

Looking around, we could see that there was no other way to observe who would come here to retrieve the money if we actually did leave any.

Chris said, "You're right. We'd have to observe who came to pick the money up from the air with a drone."

I had not been here before, and wondered where the body parts were found. Chris told me that the body parts were found up front by the welcome sign.

I wanted to confirm that the only way the two severed body parts could have gotten there was from the gulf. That would allow us to focus on who had access to the gulf. If the body parts were placed here by humans, our job would be harder.

We climbed down from the viewing tower and walked back to the parking lot. As we approached the green sign, Chris said, "In this pile of rocks is where the two body parts were found."

"Well, it's close enough to the water line that the parts could have floated in during a high tide," I said. "And, whoever tossed them into the gulf would have had no control over where they floated. They may not have even known that the body parts floated onto Green Key.

Chapter 15 – Playing Along

At 5:00 P.M. sharp, the park was almost empty except for four Pasco County Sheriff Deputies pretending to be park visitors.

A car pulled into the parking lot of Green Key and two men, sporting long beards got out of the car and headed to the boardwalk that took you out to the viewing tower.

They did not appear to be visitors as they didn't walk around the park. They just headed to the viewing tower with a single purpose in mind. And that was to retrieve the ransom money.

They got about halfway to the viewing tower along the boardwalk and then stopped. They leaned against the railing for a few minutes and then turned around and walked back to their car. Without hesitation, they then drove away.

Our drone had enough battery power to follow them out of Green Key and south to Main Street and U.S. Highway 19. At that point, the drone lost our signal, but we felt since the car turned left onto Main Street, it was probably heading toward the former Mayor of New Port Richey, Nicholas Tobias's home. But we couldn't be sure of that.

I didn't like what I was seeing. This reminded me of the kind of hide and seek the drug dealers used to play. They would pretend that they were going to do a drug deal in one spot when in actuality, they were doing it in another spot. Were they pretending to make us think that Riley was here, when really she was somewhere else.

The drone surveillance at Green Key netted nothing as no one came out to pick up the brown suitcase containing the marked one-hundred-thousand-dollars. I think they knew we had them under surveillance.

HIGH TIDE AT GREEN KEY

Was the former mayor of New Port Richey a criminal. I didn't think so. I knew he was addicted to drugs, and often hosted wild parties where drugs were used, but I didn't think he was a murderer.

HIGH TIDE AT GREEN KEY

Chapter 16 — Checking Out Marina's

"Let's begin a hunt for a boat large enough to carry four to five men. The boat would have to be at least a 27-footer, to easily hold that many people," Chris said.

"There's no boat ramp here at Green Key, so they had to take it out of the water at one of the marinas in the area. Let's check that out also," I told Chris. "It would be covered in blood," I added.

We both agreed that the two body parts must have floated in from the Gulf, and our best approach would be to hunt for a marina that the boat could have launched from or went too so it could be cleaned up.

Chris said there were two marinas in Port Richey, one in New Port Richey, and several up in Hudson Beach. Those would be where I would think a boat of this size or larger in this area would come from. There were a few watering holes along the Cotee river that a boat could have come from, but there would have been people there that saw what we suspected would be a bloody mess.

That's half-a-dozen marinas to checkout. If any of these marinas saw a boat come in with lots of blood, there would be a cleaning bill somewhere.

"I'll take the two in New Port Richey and the one in Port Richey," I said.

"Do you mind taking the ones north of here in Hudson and Sea Ranch?" I asked Chris.

"No problem," Chris responded. "But first, we need to get you back to your vehicle," he added.

After leaving the Sheriff's Office, having retrieved my Chevy Trailblazer, my first call was to a full-service marina across from Catches Waterfront Grill and just up the road from Whiskey River on The Water.

The Sunset Landing Marina is a hole-in-the-wall that not many people use. It is only about ten to fifteen minutes to Green Key Park by water from their facility, making this the one I wanted to check first.

On my way over, I called and spoke with the manager of Sunset Landing Marina, telling him I was with the Pasco County Sheriff's Office, and I needed to know if a large open fisherman, probably 27 feet or more, came in around a week ago full of blood.

He said, "There was a thirty-foot open fisherman that did come in last week. It was full of blood." The owners of the boat told him the blood was from fishing, and they wanted the boat to have a serious high-pressure cleaning, so we took care of it for them.

"There were three men on the boat that we had not seen before."

"How did they pay?" I asked.

"Their bill was $475, and they paid by credit card," he responded.

I need to stop by and get a copy of the credit card payment. Will you be there in the next half hour?" I asked.

"Not a problem," he replied. "I'll be here all afternoon. The manager said that they must have gutted a lot of fish to get that much blood on their boat.

It only took me fifteen minutes to drive the short distance to Sunset Landing Marina. It was harder to find from the street than from the water. It was right on the Cotee river.

I parked on the street next to the office. Walking in, I was greeted by the manager who asked, "Are you Jack Myers?"

"Yes," I responded. "I'm here to take a picture of the credit card receipt from the men you power washed their open fisherman boat."

"Well, I've also got them on video. We keep the camera running all day, so we know who we're dealing with. I'll get you a copy of the video," the manager said.

After taking a picture of the credit card receipt and taking a copy of the video, I got back to my car and called the other two marinas on my list. Neither of these two marinas had anything suspicious to tell me. With my chores done, I headed back to our office on Little Road.

I arrived back at the office at 3:00 P.M. and Chris got there a little past 4:00 P.M. He had gone to all four of the marinas personally to see if anyone reported anything.

"Not a thing to report," Chris said. "That

was a waste of time."

"Not for me," I said. "The manager of the first marina I went to said that three men came in on a 30' open fisherman with blood all over their boat. They paid $475 using a credit card to have the marina power wash the blood off the boat. I picked up a copy of their credit card receipt and a copy of the video that has the three men paying for the service."

"Wow, that sounds like our guys," Chris said. "What's the name on the credit card slip?"

Handing him the slip and moving to Riley's computer, I said, "Nicholas Tobias."

"Nicholas Tobias!" Chris said. "That's the former Mayor of New Port Richey. Do you think he had something to do with the murder and dismemberment of two people?" he asked. "Do a background check on him and let's see what trouble he's been in," Chris ordered me to do the research.

"I don't know what's going on in this city, but you're right, we need to find out right now," I said as I brought up the State of Florida's DEA background check system.

I've been retired for over a year, and they still show me as an active member of their department. My login capabilities are still active also.

After waiting about two minutes, Riley's computer finally came back with a profile of Nicholas Tobias, our former mayor for the past few years.

Speed reading through the report, I noticed several RELATED tags that had the name Eric Rameriz next to the tag. There were also a few PDFs on the drug investigations into Jonathan Benito, our Italian Congressman. All this was very suspicious.

After reading the background information on Nicholas Tobias, I ran facial recognition on the three men in the video from the marina that pressure cleaned the boat, to see if I could get a name. In less than a minute a name and picture popped up on the computer screen.

The name of one of the men was Jethro Bodine. The information associated with the name indicated that he had a long history of armed battery charges, along with a few charges for selling drugs.

Chapter 17 – Related Tags

Reading the history of this man, I said to Chris, "Could it be that there were two separate groups of conspirators involved in drug distribution in Pasco County?

"The first group, now in prison for the rest of their lives, was Eric and Ramone Ramirez, from the Moon Lake area. The second group and the leaders of the county's current drug distribution operation have not been incarcerated yet," I added.

"Who's that?" Chris asked.

"That would be the Congressman of our district, Jonathan Benito and the former Mayor of New Port Richey, Nicholas Tobias," I continued.

"And don't forget Sam Tobias, Nicholas

Tobias's father," Chris replied. "We may find that Nicholas's father is somehow involved in what's happening.

"We know that there were several times that the motorhome was at the same general area as Riley, which would give them an opportunity to kidnap her," Chris added.

"The motorhome was at Green Key the same time that Riley was there to interview Sam Tobias. Sam could have told his son that she was coming to interview him, and upon hearing this, the former mayor ordered Congressman Benito's aids to take the motorhome to Green Key and kidnap her there.

"The motorhome was also at the restaurant across the street from here, waiting for an opportunity to pick her up first thing in the morning.

"They were being more aggressive when

they drove onto the parking lot of the Sheriff's Office and kidnapped her there.

"That's a cool theory," I said to Chris.

"It's been three days now and we are not any closer to finding Riley. If she's in trouble, she may not be able to delay any longer."

"You're right, we need to get off our ass and find Riley, and we need to do it quick," I said. "If we don't find her soon, we're going to go from a search and rescue mode into a recovery mode," I added.

Chapter 18 – Aripeka Visit

"I going to talk with someone from Riley's past that can possibly shed some light on possible drug dealings and possible kidnappers."

"Who is that?" Chris asked me.

"His name is Tony Marino, and he now lives in Aripeka, which isn't too far away. He was an ex-Pasco-County Commissioner, an ex-State Representative, and knew Eric and Ramone Ramirez very well.

He also has a past with Riley McFarland."

Driving out to Aripeka was a treat. It was quiet and serene, and made me think of what it was like in old-time Florida. The road off of U.S. Highway 19 was narrow and full of overhanging Oak Trees. Within a hundred yards of the Gulf-of-Mexico, there was a tiny Post Office that rumor has it, Babe Ruth had used when he came here to fish.

As I approached the final bridge that connected Pasco County with Hernando County, I made a hard lefthand turn and drove to the last house on that street. The street contained six houses. The last one was Tony Marino's two-acre lot with a three-story home built on pilons. Another hundred feet and I'd have driven into the Gulf-of-Mexico.

I couldn't help but notice as I drove up to the gated driveway, that there was a thirty-foot open fisherman tied to the dock behind Tony's beautiful home.

As I came to a stop, I pushed the button at the bottom of the driveway, and immediately heard Tony's voice. The voice asked, "Who goes there?"

"Hi Tony. It's Jack Myers," I responded.

"We met in Tallahassee a little over a year ago, regarding the Rameriz family. I don't know if you are aware or not, but Riley McFarland has been kidnapped and I'm hoping you can help me with this case."

Tony responded favorably and opened the gate to allow me to pass. I drove up the long driveway and climbed the outside steps to his front door. The view was breathtaking. There was water as far as I could see.

"Jack," Tony said as he opened the front door to his beautiful home.

"Tony," I responded. "It is so great to see you again. I can understand why you retired here," I said as I gestured with my arms to the great open view.

"It is beautiful," he said. "Please, come in," he added as he led me out onto the back patio. "What is this about Riley being kidnapped?" he asked before I had a chance to even sit down.

"Yes, three days ago. We don't have many leads and I'm really concerned that if we don't get to her soon, it might be too late," I responded.

"How can I help?" he asked.

"We are tracking a large motorhome that is registered to the father of a former mayor named Nicholas Tobias. His motorhome was being driven by three younger characters, all with long hair and long beards, that were at the scene where Riley was last seen," I told Tony.

"We think this may be related to a murder investigation that Riley was working on. She might have gotten too close to the murder of two men, whose body parts washed up onto Green Key," I added.

"It looked like they were murdered out in the Gulf, and they were cut up into small pieces and dumped into the water. Two of these body parts washed ashore onto Green Key with the tide," I said to Tony.

"I know the former mayor of New Port Richey, Nicholas Tobias," Tony said. "Nicholas has always been involved in shady things, but murder?" he added. "I can't imagine him doing something like that. And I doubt his father would do something like that either.

"Yes, he owns a large motorhome, that he lets his father use to take vacations. His father goes up to Port St. Joe a lot. Sometimes, he takes Congressman Benito's three aids with him to make sure he makes it back okay or if he has any problems while out on the water."

"I just wanted you to know that Riley has been kidnapped and we need to find her. Who do you think might have taken her?" I asked. "I know you cared about her, as I did, and I hope we find her alive," I said.

"No, I don't have a clue who might have taken her, but I'll put the word out to everyone I know, and I'm sure she'll show up somewhere. Is it possible that she just took off on a binge. She's been known to do that," Tony said. "She is very unstable," he added.

"She's not like that anymore," I said in her defense. "She's more grown up now and her focus is on her job," I told Tony.

"If you think of anything, please give me a call," I said as I got up.

As I began to leave, having accomplished what I wanted, and that was to let Tony Marino know that I'm looking at him as a possible accomplice, I turned and asked Tony about his boat out back. "That's a beauty," I said. "Do you mind if I go down and admire her?" I asked.

"I'd prefer you didn't," he replied. "She's a mess from several days of fishing, and once she's cleaned up, I'll take you for a spin. There's four 250 HP outboards that can use some high-speed run time," he added.

"How far can they go on a long run without having to refuel?" I asked.

"I've taken them out into the Gulf-of-Mexico and made it to Panama City with a stopover in Cedar Key to refuel. But that's when the weather is good and the gulf is calm," Tony responded.

Tony then walked me to the door and made sure I left.

I didn't think that Tony would do anything to harm Riley, so I chalked this one up to a man with a boat. His feeling about the former mayor was helpful also.

HIGH TIDE AT GREEN KEY

Chapter 19 – Crew Lake Wilderness Park

Riley opened her eyes and could tell she had been drugged. What she didn't know was that she was out in the wilderness and left to be eaten by the alligators and poisoned by the water moccasins. She had been given cocaine and meth, chained, and left unconscious.

It was almost a full day that she had been unconscious. Coming too, she rubbed her eyes and then in a moment of severe pain, grabbed her leg.

Attached to her leg as a huge metal device with large teeth on it that was beginning to dig into her skin. The more she moved, the more the device dug into her leg.

She was lying next to a concrete boat ramp that was once used to allow boat trailers to unload their watercraft into Crew Lake.

The lake had long been abandoned, as the water level had dropped too many feet to be safe, and the lake was full of weeds, Lilypad's, and other growth. Looking around, she could tell that she was chained to a Department of Transportation sign that had been knocked over.

The sign had three arrows on it that looked like sideway letter V's. Obviously, the sign pointed boats to the left many years ago, but it was out of place and the lake didn't have much water in it.

There was no boat traffic out here in the middle of nowhere. Riley could only hear the sound of alligators in the distance. Her body was dirty and sweaty, and her leg was bloody.

With no cellphone, she had no way of calling for help.

"Jack, I beg you. Please come find me,"

PART II

HIGH TIDE AT GREEN KEY

Chapter 20 – Allyson Myers Case

After my visit with Tony Marino, I headed back to the Sheriff's Office on Little Road. I knew we needed to begin an all-out effort to find Riley, soon, but I wanted to do some research into what law enforcement had accomplished this past year regarding the murder of my wife.

It was already past 8:00 P.M., and most of the clerical staff had gone home. There were a few deputies still doing research on finding Riley, but they didn't pay any attention to me. I knew in the morning that we would begin with a visit to the Congressman's home, and hopefully that would lead to Riley.

I logged onto Riley's computer and brought up the Allyson Myers case. In re-reading the report, it began with a summary that indicated Allyson Myers was murdered at Moon Lake Park at the beginning of the summer of last year. The report also indicated that she was clubbed to death by a large object such as a baseball bat or a four-by-four hunk of wood. The report continued by indicating that drugs appeared to be involved as Fentanyl pills were found around the body.

I read about the condition of her body, and that's when the report mentioned my name as the husband, and a possible suspect. Other suspects were noted as homeless inhabitants of the park. Several homeless people were interviewed, and one said they believed the murderer was a female because of the upward swinging of the murder weapon and the small thin posture of the murderer.

The coroner's report indicated the blows to the head were made in an upward swing, like that from a kid or a woman, rather than in a downward swing like that from a large man.

What this report did tell me was that if Eric had killed my wife, he would have been immediately recognized by those who lived at the park because of his size and demeaner. Eric did not look like a woman. He was an overweight big person.

My gut told me that the murderer was a woman or short slender man from the homeless group that lived at the park.

The report did tell of Eric having a female accomplice who kept him happy. I suspected Riley of being Eric's accomplice but had no proof. This would be something I would try to obtain down the road.

I also thought that whoever wanted Riley kidnapped, could have done so because she was instrumental in having Eric arrested. He was a well-known distributor of drugs.

Chapter 21 – Nighttime Run

The Coast Guard had met with the Pasco County Sheriff's Office this past week to provide us with information about a drug smuggling operation that was underway between Port St. Joe, Florida, and Pasco County.

They believed Fentanyl was finding its way down to our area using small boats traveling along the coastline at night.

We had Tony Marino's thirty-foot open fisherman and Nicholas Tobias twenty-seven-foot open fisherman under surveillance for the past twenty-four hours and neither has moved.

Then just after sunset last night, to our surprise, Tony Marino loaded his thirty-foot open fisherman with five coolers and took it out into the gulf. The Coast Guard monitored his journey from the air and kept us informed about his destination. They weren't much help however, as they lost him after an hour as they had to turn around and refuel.

St. Joe was about a ten-hour trip, covering around three-hundred miles, so we knew that Tony's open fisherman could handle that journey with only one stop for refueling.

My initial conclusions about Tony Marino were wrong. It appeared that our Coast Guard caught him on his way to Port St. Joe, to pick up a load of Fentanyl and Cocaine. He was apprehended with five coolers full of drugs on his return trip as soon as he made a refueling stop at Cedar Key.

Tony's first call was to his lawyer and his next call was to whoever he was picking up the drugs from Port St. Joe for. His message to a man known as Jethro Bodine, one of Congressman Benito's three aids, was, "not going to make dinner tonight. You need to get dinner on your own."

I'm sure that was a coded message of some sort. Since Tony lawyered up, and was released on bail pending a hearing, he had nothing to say.

What I did know was that he was involved in the Florida drug business but had nothing to do with the kidnapping of Riley. He cared too much for her.

Chapter 22 – Bending the Rules

Seeing that we had enough information for a search warrant, Chris phoned in a request to the County Court Commissioner for our district for a search warrant for the former mayor's home in New Port Richey. We had probable cause, and the request was to search for drugs or clues to the kidnapping of Riley McFarland.

We had to do it this way as Judges didn't really work after 5:00 P.M.

The judge denied the request for a search warrant because he felt there was not sufficient evidence to warrant an evasion of privacy.

I guess there was some favors being returned there.

"Don't be too upset Chris," I said to him. "We'll just collect more evidence and resubmit our request in a day or two.

"Right now, our main focus must be to find Riley," I said in a concerning tone. "I know it's late, but let's drive down to Congressman Benito's home in Tarpon Springs. I'd like to talk to him and his assistants," I said to Chris.

"We don't have a warrant. Shouldn't we call first?" he asked. "He may not even be there now."

"That's even more reason to go now. Surprise is our best weapon. Actually, I don't want to talk with him. It's his assistants I want to talk with. He has three of them, and I'm beginning to think they had a lot to do with Riley's kidnapping."

Congressman Jonathan Benito lived in Tarpon Springs on one of the many lakes that made up that community. His large home was not gated, so we drove right up onto his driveway, which rapped around to the back of the house.

As we were getting out of the car, a tall, long haired, and bearded young Greek man came out and greeted us.

"The Congressman is not here now," he said. "If you'd like to make an appointment, I can take your information," he added.

"That's okay," I replied. "it's you we'd really like to talk with," I said. "I'm Jack Myers and this is Chris Duncan and we're with the Pasco County Sheriff's Office. Can you give us a minute of your time?" I asked.

"What's this all about," he asked. "You're a little out of your jurisdiction," he added.

"What were you doing at Green Key three days ago?" I asked.

"I was with my two brothers," he replied. "We were going to see the sunset. Why do you ask?"

"Are your brothers here now?" I followed his response.

"Sure, they're inside.

"Can we come in and talk with them?" I said in a commanding voice.

"No, but I'll have them come out and talk with you," he replied.

"What's your name?" I asked snapping a quick picture of him with my cellphone.

"I'm Jethro," he responded. "My two brothers are Jeremy and Jake. I'll go get them and we'll be right out," he said as he went back inside the house.

I added Jethro's name to his picture I just took. As I put his name into my cellphone, the three of them all came outside.

HIGH TIDE AT GREEN KEY

"As you know, I'm Jethro Bodine," he began. "My brothers are Jeremy and Jake, pointing to them respectively. What would you like to know?" he asked.

"What was the real reason you were out at Green Key earlier this week?" I asked.

"Like I said," Jethro responded. "We wanted to see the sunset out over the Gulf-of-Mexico."

"That's bullshit," I responded. "Three young men don't go out to watch the sunset without beer or joints, and you certainly didn't drink beer at that park," I said in a raised voice. "Did you go out there to kidnap Riley McFarland?"

Jeremy and Jake looked at each other and then conferred with Jeremy. After a few seconds, the three brothers asked to talk off the record.

"We need to make sure what we tell you will not result in us going to prison for kidnapping.

"We don't want to spend the rest of our lives behind bars," Jeremy said to me in a soft voice, speaking on behalf of the three brothers.

"Tell me what you did, and what you know, and I'll make sure that you don't go to prison for kidnapping. You may go to prison for murder if Riley is not found alive however," I said to the three of them in a clear and firm voice.

"Congressman Jonathan Benito ordered us to go to Green Key and kidnap the female deputy who was there to talk with the former mayor's father, Sam Tobias. He told us to put her into the motorhome and bring her here. That's why we were going to Green Key.

"The Congressman was told she would be there just before sunset," Jeremy said as he looked directly into my eyes. "Because of a roadside incident, we were not able to accomplish our goal.

"The next day, we told the Congressman what happened, and he ordered us to wait out front of the Breakfast Station restaurant across the street from the Sheriff's Office, since she was a regular patron there. He told us to pick her up there. We watched for her for a couple of days, but she never showed up.

"Then, the day we kidnapped her, she was there, but with two other men. We decided not to act and drove across the street to the parking lot of the Sheriff's office. When she came out, that's when we grabbed her and drove back here," Jethro added.

"Congressman Benito interrogated her about what she knew, but she didn't know anything about any murders. That's when he ordered us to take her to a place where she'd not be found.

We contacted Sam and he led us out to Pasco County's Crew Lake Wilderness Park. Sam told us no one would ever find her there," Jake chimed in. "We didn't even know where we were or what this place was," Jethro said.

"Is that where she's at now?" I said in a loud voice.

"If she's still alive, that's what I would think," Jethro said.

"Alright, get in," I said to the three of them pointing to my rented Chevy Trailblazer.

"Unless you arrest us, we can't leave Congressman Benito's home. We're obligated by law to remain here in case he comes home. We are employees of the Federal Government and need their permission to vacate our duty," Jake said. Jethro felt that the local Sheriff's Office couldn't interrogate the congressman since he had diplomatic immunity.

"Then tell us where at Crew Lake, you put Riley," I demanded.

"She's chained to an old DOT sign at the end of a boat ramp that is not used anymore," Jethro told us.

Based on the information provided by congressman Benito's assistants, we headed east to hunt for the whereabouts of Riley McFarland at Crew Lake Wilderness Park.

Crew Lake was just north of State Road 52 and east of the Veteran's Highway. By the time we got there, it was 8:00 P.M. and almost dark.

"Shit," I said. "We should have made one of the congressman's aids come with us, to show where they took her. If we don't find her tonight, we'll arrest the three brothers first thing in the morning and force them to show us where they put her.

What we didn't know was that Riley was

attached to a bear trap in the middle of Crew Lake Wilderness Park at its one of many boat ramps. And, at this time of year, the park was full of alligators and other predators. All of them hungry and looking for food.

Chapter 23 – The Hunt Begins

We pulled into the main entrance to the Crew Lake Wilderness Park. The sign said the park closed at dusk, so we knew we only had less than an hour to find the boat ramp and Riley McFarland.

Located in north central Pasco County near the Suncoast Parkway, Crews Lake Wilderness Park covers 113 acres along the west shore of a mostly dried up Lake. The lake is the headwaters of the larger Pithlachascotee River that flows into the Gulf of Mexico 25 miles downstream. There is access for fishing and kayaking at Crew Lake, but the lake level can vary by extremes depending on total annual rainfall. It has been known to be completely dry in periods of severe drought. Lake level is also affected by the presence of numerous sinkholes that drain into the

Floridan aquifer, and from groundwater wellfield pumping.

The park includes hiking trails, a short, paved bike trail, a playground, a wooden tower, athletic fields, and a miniature Central Pasco & Gulf Railroad line that offers rides on the miniature railroad twice a month.

Crews Lake, along with Moon Lake, reached its lowest recorded water level in 2009 before slowly regaining some depth with heavier rains in the summer of 2010.

The lake has recovered further due to the rains produced by Tropical Storm Debby in 2012, up to the point of flooding dirt pathways and areas near pavilions, as of October 2016.

As we drove through the park, there were at least a dozen side roads that we could choose to take. Some had signs that indicated a pavilion number, but some roads didn't indicate where they would lead to.

We ventured down some of these roads, only to arrive at a dead-end.

We were looking for a boat ramp, so we tried to drive along the lake. Off in the distance, we could see gators swimming in the lake and some resting on the banks of the lake.

As I entered each roadway, I wondered how hard I really wanted to find Riley. Did she kill my wife? Was she that desperate to have me all to herself? If she was responsible, I don't think I could live with her.

Chapter 24 – The Rescue

Earlier in the day, Riley tried to climb to the top of the traffic sign, but the chain attached to the bear trap wasn't long enough to allow that to happen.

Lying there in the water, she thought that it had been several days since she was kidnapped. She presumed that they held her captive for at least a day while they figured out what to do with her. Once they decided, it probably took another half-a-day to drug her and bring her to where she currently was at. She guessed that she had been at the lake for close to three days.

Tonight was probably going to be her last as she was losing strength, she hadn't had any food or water, and the alligators were coming closer and closer.

She had hoped someone would come to use the boat ramp and find her lying there. But the six-inch thick concrete ramp ended up two feet above the current water level. No one would use this ramp. Probably no one would come to this part of the park.

What she did know was that she was becoming dehydrated, and hungry. Without water that was drinkable, she knew she only had another day to live. That is if she was allowed to live given the predators that came out in search of food every night. She was the food that they hunted.

As nighttime approached, Riley feared the dark. She knew this evening could be her last. She had nothing to protect herself with and couldn't do much to move around since the bear trap was cutting into her leg.

To make matters worse, she was losing blood. The physical discomfort Riley felt was nowhere near the fear and desperation she was going through. She could feel her heart rate was elevated, and she was beginning to feel shortness of breath.

==================

After searching for about 45 minutes, Chris and I saw a signpost with an arrow pointing off to the left that read boat ramp. Following the arrow down the road that the arrow instructed, for another five minutes, we reached another signpost that read "pull your boat in here and back it down the ramp".

Chris and I jumped out of our vehicle and ran down to the boat ramp. At the end of the ramp, we saw Riley, lying with her head in a foot of water, and barely alive.

It took a couple of bullets from my gun to break open the bear trap and free her leg. Severely cut and bleeding, we knew she wouldn't be able to walk to my car. Chris and I held her up, with one of her arms around our shoulder, as we started to walk back to my vehicle.

All of a sudden, we stopped in our tracks. Lying between us and my SUV, was an eight-foot alligator, and it was looking at us for its next meal.

We didn't move. We guessed the alligator was probably on his way to Riley.

Chris said in an almost screaming and panicked voice, "Shoot the mother fucker."

I wasn't sure if that was legal or not, but now was not the time for legalities. I pulled out my gun and made sure it had a bullet ready to fire. Then without further hesitation, we scooted along the alligator's tail and got behind it. I then fired my gun and put a bullet into the back of its head.

The alligator grunted and dropped its head to the ground. Not waiting for anything else to happen, we hurried as fast as we could to my SUV. We lifted Riley into the back seat and then we jumped into the front seats.

Just as we were getting ready to rush out of the park, a ranger's vehicle pulled alongside of us and told us it was time to leave the park as it was closing for the night.

I could see the Ranger noticed the alligator lying on the ground behind my vehicle, but we didn't wait around to tell them our story.

I thanked him for checking on us and told him what a wonderful park this was. Then without wasting another second, I put the SUV in gear and took off.

HIGH TIDE AT GREEN KEY

PART III

HIGH TIDE AT GREEN KEY

Chapter 25 – Riley is Back Involved

I took Riley to Bayonet Point Hospital to be checked out and have her leg stitched up, but she didn't want to stay there long.

Chris and I took her home after being at the hospital only half a day and told her to get some rest. We said one of us would come pick her up in the morning and get as much sleep as she could.

The next morning, Chris picked Riley up and brought her into the office. We spent the rest of the day bringing her up to speed on the status of this case. Things were beginning to come together, with regard to the Green Key murders.

We told Riley we had our sites on two rather well-to-do politicians of being involved in a drug smuggling operation. We think that the two murders are related to this drug smuggling operation and the murder may have occurred during the handoff of Fentanyl out in the gulf.

What we couldn't figure out was why would either of the two long time politicians we suspected, kill two members of their team because they got a little handsy with the merchandise. They couldn't be that greedy.

We explained to Riley that we felt comfortable thinking that the murder of two people occurred on a good-sized boat, probably an open fisherman. We think the body parts were thrown into the water so there would be no trace of the two victims. What our suspects didn't expect was that two of the body parts would float in with the tide onto Green Key.

Having been away from the case for several days, Riley's mind was fresh, and she saw things a little differently.

HIGH TIDE AT GREEN KEY

"What if the killer was not one of these two suspected drug traffickers?" Riley said. It doesn't make sense that these two prominent men would jeopardize their positions or reputation by killing a couple of petty thieves.

"What if it were someone, not from here, that didn't know the tidal changes in the gulf. If our killer didn't know that in the Gulf-of-Mexico, the tide level usually changes only once a day if the moon is in a certain position, and only rose or fell about one meter at that," Riley added.

"If they'd have known, they wouldn't have killed these two people so close to shore and thrown their body parts into the water."

"Whoever killed these two men had a rather large boat and they weren't afraid of performing gruesome acts upon others," I said to her.

Keeping with our suspicions, we knew that Congressman Benito and Tony Marino both had rather large open fisherman boats.

"Tomorrow morning," I said, "Congressman Jonathan Benito is coming in to talk with us. So, I think it will be a good opportunity to find out what he knows and what he confirms. And what he can tell us about his 30-foot open fisherman being pressure washed at a marina, with lots of blood all over it.

Riley said she was getting tired, and wondered if one of us would take her home. Chris offered, but said he had to pick his wife up at the dentist, so he suggested me as her chauffer. He was leaving early, and he had the day off tomorrow.

I didn't like the idea of carrying Riley into her apartment and putting her in her bed, without someone else being there.

I grabbed a wheelchair from the back room

of the Sheriff's Office and wheeled Riley out to my SUV. After getting her into my SUV and loading the wheelchair into the back, I took her home.

Fifteen minutes later, we were at Riley's apartment, and with a little difficulty, I carried her up to her 2nd floor walkup. We had to leave the wheelchair behind so I decided I would come back for it once I carried her into her bedroom and put her into her bed.

As I did, with her arms around my neck, she forced me down onto the bed. "You can take me if you want," she said.

I looked into her eyes and said, "You are so gorgeous. I'd love to make love to you, but I'm afraid you're in no condition for that kind of ruckus."

"Try me," she said. She then lifted her head and kissed me firmly on the lips. My arms were all over her as she rolled over and was on top of me. I could tell she was feeling no pain.

I unbuttoned her blouse and rubbed my hands all over the front of her. She was breathing heavily.

Just as I was about ready to unclip her bra, my cell phone rang. Without thinking, I rolled over and answered it.

"Yes Congressman Benito," I said. "Our meeting is at 9:00 A.M. tomorrow morning. Yes, see you then," I said.

With that, I got out of Riley's bed and straightened my clothes. I was still showing some effects from my short roll in the hay.

Feeling that was a sign from above, I left her alone in her bed and went down to get her wheelchair.

As I walked by her SUV, I looked inside Riley's SUV and noticed something on the rear passenger seat. It was a large four-by-four hunk of wood. I wondered what she was doing with that in her vehicle.

HIGH TIDE AT GREEN KEY

Chapter 26 – Interviewing the Congressman

Early the next morning, I stopped by Riley's apartment and picked her up. She had already showered and dressed and was ready to leave.

"I thought you might stay the night and help me dress this morning," Riley said to me with a smile.

"You were all over me, and once Congressman Benito called to confirm the time of our meeting, I had lost the urge," I responded.

"I saw your urge," she said. "Oh baby, you hadn't lost your urge," she giggled.

When we got to the office, she asked me to go across the street and bring back a couple of coffees, which I readily did.

Congressman Jonathan Benito was due in for an interrogation at 9:00 A.M., sharp, so we needed to get ready with our list of questions for him. If he has nothing to fear, he'll provide us with the information about his boat.

The Congressman was not very happy with being dragged to our office on Little Road so early in the morning. He came with his three aids, but they weren't allowed into the interrogation room. It was just him, me, and Riley.

"Okay," he said, "let's get this over with. I've got more important things to do today than talk with you assholes," he added.

"Good morning Congressman Benito," Riley said. I guess you know who I am? This should take only a few minutes, so relax," she added.

"Just make it quick," he said as he moved across the room and sat in the chair that was in the corner. "I guess this is where you want me to sit?" he asked.

"Congressman Benito," I began, "who was the last person you gave permission to use your thirty-foot open fisherman?" Riley asked.

"It was my three aids, about a week ago, to go fishing in the gulf waters. It was their day off," he answered.

"That would be Jethro, Jeremy, and Jake Bodine?" Riley asked.

"Yes, you already know their names," he said in anger.

"And did they bring back any fish?" Riley asked sarcastically.

"Yes, a ton of Tiger Fish and a lot of Tarpon," he answered. They cleaned the fish on the boat before returning to shore. Being good aids, they went and had the boat cleaned before returning it to my storage rack. I think there was a charge of just under $500 that I paid on my credit card."

Riley could see that Congressman Benito was getting angry with these stupid questions, so Riley cut right to the chase.

"Why did you order your aids to kidnap me and take me to Crew Lake Wilderness Park?" she asked.

"I did no such thing," Congressman Benito responded. "Do I need a lawyer?" he asked.

"Your aids told me that you ordered them to kidnap me. Are you saying that they are lying?" she asked.

"I don't know anything about a kidnapping," he responded. I certainly don't do that kind of thing," he added.

Riley summarized our case, "We are working on the murder of two men that were killed on a large boat and their body parts were thrown into the gulf waters. Two of those body parts floated ashore onto Green Key. We think that whoever was involved in that heinous act tried to kidnap me for getting to close to finding out who did this and had me kidnapped."

"Well, it wasn't me and if my three aids did this, it was their day off, so I don't know anything about it," he responded.

"Is that it?" the Congressman said. "You made me come all the way down here because the three men that work for me went fishing in my boat. I'll be talking with Sheriff Nocco about this," he said. "Can I go now?"

We released him and chose not to talk with his three aids at this time.

HIGH TIDE AT GREEN KEY

Chapter 27 – A Cast of Possibilities

Riley was pissed that Congressman Benito wouldn't take the bait and be responsible for her kidnapping.

Although her kidnappers covered her head with a cloth bag, she presumed that she was taken to his home in Tarpon Springs, and it was his three aids that took her to Crew Lake.

I just sat back and observed the whole thing. I felt that Riley exposed too much and gave Congressman Benito a way out.

So where were we, I thought to myself. The cast of possibilities were the Congressman, or his aids, Tony Marino, or someone we haven't thought of yet. My money was on the three aids. But, they had no reason to kidnap Riley or kill two guys in the gulf unless they were paid an ungodly amount of money. An amount they couldn't resist. No other suspect made sense.

Riley was still sitting in the interrogation room after Congressman Jonathan Benito left the Sheriff's Office. His last words were that the Sheriff would hear about this huge waste of time.

Chapter 28 – Taking a Break

"Let's get out of here and get a drink," Riley suggested.

"That should help put our minds in the right frame of mind to come up with something concrete," I said.

"Where to?" she asked.

"Let's go back to my hotel," I responded. "We can sit out on the balcony and look out over the bay. That should put us in the right frame of mind. Then we can have dinner somewhere downtown," I added. "I'll take you home afterwards."

"Really!," she responded with a lot of doubt in her voice.

An hour later, we were at my hotel room, looking out over Tampa Bay. The lights of the city were bright, and the night was warm. The hotel room I booked was on the twelfth floor and faced Tampa Bay. Going to the bar in my room, I asked, "Do you still drink Amaretto and Club Soda?"

"You remembered," she said with a smile.

Happy with my memory, I fixed her a drink and poured myself a bourbon on the rocks. Then I turned on some soft music on my cell phone and brought both our drinks out onto the balcony.

"What a view," she continued as she leaned on the railing.

I put my hand on her shoulder and gave Riley a big hug and a kiss on the back of the neck.

"You need to stop that, or we'll never make it to dinner," she said.

"Maybe I want you for dinner," I replied.

She turned and leaned into me, and I kissed her real hard. The weather was warm and so were the both of us. After a few minutes of kissing and hugging, we separated and went back inside to sit on the couch.

"Wow, that was close," she said. "Another minute and I would have completely given in to you," she added.

"Another minute and I would have had you naked on the balcony," I said catching my breath.

"How about that dinner," Riley asked. "We really need to work on how best to proceed with this case."

"You're right," I responded. "Stupid me for thinking sex with you would be more fun."

We got up and rode the elevator down to the lobby. Stepping out of the elevator, I said, "We should still make finding a large boat, possibly with blood still all over its hull, our main priority. I would think that should lead us to the killers."

"Do you think the three brothers are involved?" Riley asked..

"Okay, I'm starving," I said. "Can we continue this over dinner? Where do you want to go for dinner? It's on the County tonight," I added.

"How about the Rusty Pelican?" Riley said.

"Perfect," I said. "Let's walk."

We left the Grand Hyatt and held hands as we walked along the causeway to the Rusty Pelican. I could tell Riley was really enjoying this evening. It had been a long time since she held hands with someone and walked under the stars and the moon.

As we got close to the Rusty Pelican, a barrage of shots rang out from behind us. One of the bullets just missed Riley and hit the car that was parked alongside where we were standing.

"What the Fuck," I said. Instinctively, I

grabbed Riley and forced her to the ground. I laid on top of her to protect her from another bullet coming our way. "Are you okay?" I asked as I raised her head up from ground. "Are you hit?"

"I'm fine," she replied. "What was that?

"I don't know, but we're going to find out," I said. "I called 911 from my cell phone and reported the shots. Wait here," I said as I got up and ran in the direction of the shots.

Within a few moments, two sheriff's cars came racing by with their sirens and lights flashing. They stopped exactly where we were standing.

"It's okay," one of them said. "There was a robbery and mugging on the next block, and apparently one of the robbers fired some shots indiscriminately into the air," the cop continued.

"I did see a man running away when I got to the corner," I said to the cop, "but I couldn't tell who it was. I do know that the man was tall and well built."

With that explanation, I turned to Riley and said, "I don't know, but I'm thinking we may want to just leave the area. How about if I take you home now?" I said.

"I'd rather stay with you tonight," she replied. "I'm a little shaken, and I won't feel safe by myself."

"I could see she was visibly upset, I thought to myself." It was time for me to shit or get off the pot, as the saying goes. Was I going to remain loyal to Paola or was I going to stay the player I always was.

They say a leopard never changes its spots, and I needed a decision. Take Riley home or take her to my hotel room.

I made my decision, and we took the elevator back up to my room. "I'll just order room service," I said to her. Once back in my hotel room, I ordered dinner for the both of us.

After dinner and a bottle of wine, Riley and I sat out on the balcony. I held her close to me and I could feel her body sink into mine. She was still upset, but relaxed.

As we sat on the balcony, she stood up and began to undress. I began to kiss her all over. She was unsteady on her feet, having just been shot at, as she flopped back onto the lounge chair. She laid their naked and pointed at me to undress and join her. I did as she enjoyed watching me follow her command.

Riley got up and went over to the railing. The moon glistened on the bay and also on her naked body. I joined her as we made our way back to the bedroom.

Riley looked into my eyes, and said, "Only love can hurt like this."

Chapter 29– The Pieces Begin to Fall Together

The next morning, Riley and I drove directly from the hotel to the Sherrif's office so she could get her car. She then drove it across the street to the restaurant as if she was coming from her home.

It was 7:30 A.M., and the time we normally all met at the Breakfast Station. Chris was actually a little early and had a booth for us.

I walked in and saw Chris sitting in the corner. I walked over and said, "Good morning Chris," as I slid into his booth. I didn't want to say anything about what happened last night, but he did look a lot like the person who shot at Riley and me.

Just as I slid in, Riley walked into the restaurant and came directly over to where we were sitting. "Good morning, Chris, good morning Jack," she said as she motioned to the waitress to bring two coffees.

As she slid into the booth next to me, I said, "I guess you saw me walk in just ahead of you and assumed that I hadn't ordered coffee yet." I didn't think we were fooling Chris who just looked at us and smiled.

"How was your day off?" she asked Chris trying to make light conversation and ignored my comment.

"It was all work," he responded. "I'm glad I was able to get the time off. I got a lot done."

Later today, we have a SWAT team ready to search the former Mayor's home. "I'd like to go with Jack when he executes that search. Will that be okay?" Chris asked.

"Sure, why not?" Riley said.

HIGH TIDE AT GREEN KEY

We ordered breakfast and ate as quietly as possible. Afterward, we got back into our vehicles and drove across the street to the Sheriff's Office building.

"So, how did the interrogation of Congressman Benito go?" Chris asked.

"It didn't go well," I responded. "He denied everything his aids told us, and he said he didn't know anything about any murders."

"Did you talk to his three aids?" Chris asked in a concerning tone.

"No, they didn't stick around long enough for us to do that," Riley said.

"Has the coroner released an updated report on the two body parts found on Green Key?" I asked Riley.

"Not since we last looked at it," she responded.

Later that day, when Jack and Chris

returned from executing the search warrant on the former Mayor's home, I turned to Riley and asked, "Why don't you bring it up on your computer and we'll check to see if it's been updated," I said.

"There was nothing new in the Medical Examiner's report," Riley said looking it over. She Re-read the screen and said it read the same as it had a few days ago.

I moved to the chair next to Riley and said, "Do a background check on the two victims of our murder case. There must be something there."

"You mean Aaron Russo and David Russo?" she asked.

"Do we know of any other victims in this case?" I sarcastically responded.

Riley just looked at me and said, "You've gotten meaner since you've been away. You never treated me like this," she said.

HIGH TIDE AT GREEN KEY

She then pressed some buttons and did a background search of these two names and was shocked at what was there. "Holy Shit," she said out loud. "Jack, do you see what I see?"

Chapter 30 – Informant's Revenge

The background check noted that Aaron Russo and David Russo were from the New York area, but their last known address was in Baltimore. It says on this background PDF that they were informants for a Baltimore DEA Agent named Chris Duncan.

You just went to the former Mayor's home to execute a search warrant with Chris," she said.

"And it didn't go well," I responded. "Sam Tobias committed suicide there. He was apparently hiding in his son's home."

"Look here, Riley said. "It says here the Bureau have these two informants in protective custody here in Florida, preparing them to be witness's against the man they worked for.

"Can you believe this," Riley shouted out. "This is incredible. The two brothers that were mutilated were Chris's informants," she said with a laugh. "It's all too funny.

"I'll bet he came down here to Florida to kill them," she said.

"I'm going to try something," she jumped up forgetting that her leg had severe wounds and fell back into her chair.

"What are you going to do?" I asked Riley.

"I'll handle this," she said as she pulled out her cell phone and dialed the Baltimore Drug Enforcement Administration number that Pasco County had for law enforcement calls.

The DEA's office answered and promptly asked if they could put her on hold. Two minutes later, they came back on the line.

"Baltimore DEA," the man answering the

phone said. "How may I help you?"

"Hi," she began. "My name is Riley McFarland and I'm with the Pasco County Sheriff's Office, here in Florida. I'm calling to speak with an old friend named Chris Duncan. Can you put me through to him?" she said.

"I'm sorry Ma'am," the voice on the other end responded. "Chris is on vacation. Can I send him a text with a number of where to reach you?" the man answering the call asked.

Riley thought for a moment, and then decided to put Chris on notice. She gave the man in Baltimore her cell phone number and her name.

"Now we just need to wait for him to call," she said to me.

Chris, who came into the room was antsy and jumped to his feet when his cell phone buzzed, indicating he had a text message from his Baltimore office with Riley's name and number on it. After reading the text message, he said, "Okay, let's cut the bullshit."

Riley broke the ice and said, "I think you are the person that killed the Russo brothers.

"And then you paid the three aids of Congressman Benito to kidnap me because you thought I was getting to close to solving the case. How much did you pay them to do that?" she shouted.

I could tell that Chris was mad and he didn't want to go to prison for the murders that occurred out in the gulf. He knew he'd end up alongside those he's already sent to prison.

"Since you don't have any proof of this, and all your accusations are false, I'm stopping my training with the Pasco County Sheriff's Office, packing up my stuff here, and heading home. As soon as we pack up there, I'll be driving back to Baltimore."

Riley said, "Hold on Chris. You're not going anywhere except to jail. You're under arrest for ordering the murder of Aaron Russo and David Russo. And because of what you did to their bodies, this murder has diabolical circumstances, so the death penalty could be your fate.

"If you make it easier on us, we could make it easier for you," Riley said. "Please feel free to fill in all the missing pieces of this case.

"Based on the money trail," Riley continued, "we know you paid Sam Tobias two-hundred thousand dollars to come with you on the boat and kill your Baltimore informants.

"I checked and your two informants were getting ready to expose you for stealing a million dollars of drug money in Baltimore.

They already made a video of their testimony, which is currently in the hands of Baltimore prosecutors. So, killing them did not help your cause.

"We also know it was your boat that went out into the gulf the night the murders occurred. You had Sam and your two informants with you. We checked and you own a twenty-seven foot open fisherman that you keep at the house you are renting."

"We're told by a neighbor that you spent hours cleaning the blood off your boat after your return from disposing of the bodies you cut up. You had all this planned and brought your boat down to Florida exactly for this purpose," she said.

"In summary, you put your boat into the gulf somewhere near Green Key and took Sam Tobias along as your guide. His job was also to watch your two informants while you drove the boat. Once he killed them, you cut up the bodies and dumped them into the gulf. Then you returned home and cleaned yourself up and your boat.

"You're crazy," Chris said. "You have no proof of this," he added.

"Yes I do," Riley said. "I have a recording that I was able to make while being held captive by Congressman Benito three aids.

"I secretly used my smart watch to record Sam Tobias telling Jethro that you cut up the Russo Brothers after he, Sam, killed them for you. Sam said you offered him two hundred thousand dollars to kill the two informants while on the boat.

"Sam added that you ordered Jethro to take me somewhere I'd never be found. He said that you were worried I would discover your role in all this."

Riley had one question for Chris before they took him away. She asked, "Why did you tape his eyes open?" she asked.

"Because he wasn't quite dead yet and I wanted him to see me cutting his head off," Chris answered.

With that, two officers who were waiting in the office came up took Chris's two guns, along with his badge, and put him in handcuffs. "I'll get you for this," Chris shouted as they took him to a holding cell. "Your recording is not admissible in court," he yelled.

The next day, the Federal Government stepped in and took Chris Duncan to a Federal Holding Facility. He was charged with conspiracy to commit murder, and conspiracy to kidnap a Law Enforcement Officer. These were some of the charges that were being made against Chris Duncan.

Riley knew that attorneys would have a field day with this case, and she didn't have much hope of all of it sticking. But some of it would. What she did know was that Chris would never be able to return to work in the field of law enforcement again.

As it turned out, Chris walked out of the Federal Holding Facility, on his own recognizance, and returned to his Florida home.

Riley had her recording transcribed into a written report and sent it, along with other testimony, to Baltimore's lead prosecutor.

Chris was finally taken by Federal Officers back to Baltimore, along with his boat.

Riley and I went to see him off because we wanted to take pictures of his twenty-seven foot open fisherman the Feds were towing.

==============

Riley was congratulated on her handling of the case and promoted to Detective. At the party in celebration of her promotion, I asked Riley, "How did you get all this information from Jethro, that you had on Chris?"

I was in control of Jethro," she responded with a laugh. "He was weak. All you men are. All I had to do was arouse him sexually and he'd do anything I asked."

Of course, all that she said about how she obtained this information was fake. She really did obtain this by using her smart watch, not seducing Jethro. She was playing with me as I had heard these exact words from her before.

I also asked Riley about the night Chris tagged along with the SWAT team that raided the former mayor's home.

"That was something that Chris set up," she responded. "Chris convinced a judge to issue a search warrant on the former mayor's home, and then told Sam that his son was out of town and that he needed to be at the home when the SWAT team arrived. They wanted to search the house for drugs.

Riley continued, "Chris knew that Sam would be the only one in the house, and Chris killed him to make it look like a suicide. Jethro told me that Sam knew too much for his own good."

Pouring myself another drink, I thought to myself, Chris was an evil man, who only cared about money. I wonder if being a DEA Agent in Baltimore made him that way.

"Pour me one also," Riley said as she approached, and leaned up against me.

"I guess I'm easy, like most men, so are you going to sexually arouse me to force me to make you another drink?" I asked. I was being very sarcastic.

"What are you going to do now, Jack?" Riley asked changing the subject, as she took a sip from the drink I made her. "Are you going back to Puerto Rico, to be with your little girlfriend, or are you staying here in Florida?

"I've decided to stay here and hunt for my wife's killer. It's looking more and more like a woman killed her," I responded. "So, that means I'll be staying here for a while," I added.

Well, I hope you find a nice place to live. You cannot stay with me," Riley said. "I've finally made Detective, and I'm not going to take a chance on going back to my evil ways."

"You think I will cause you to go back to your evil ways?" I said with a smile on my face. "If that's what you think, it's not true."

"Anyway, I'll always be around to watch over you," I said as I leaned over and gave her a kiss in front of everyone.

I chose not to mention the four-by-four in the back seat of her SUV.

The End

BOOKS BY BEN REINHART

MURDER MYSTERIES

- Murder on Moon Lake *(Book 1)*
- High Tide at Green Key *(Book 2)*

www.amazon.com/author/benreinhart

BOOKS BY BEN REINHART

CHILDRENS BOOKS
(The Adventures of Sugar and Spice)

- Where Do Snowbirds Go?
- Are you the Easter Bunny?
- All we want for Christmas is...
- Day at the Groomer
- Our Summer Vacation
- A Dog with No Name
- Cooper & Rosey's Wedding
- The Rainbow Bridge
- It's Just a Hurricane

www.amazon.com/author/benreinhart

BOOKS BY BEN REINHART

TERRORIST STORIES

The King Maker Trilogy

- The King Maker
- The Knights of Freedom
- The Winds of Change

FBI Agent Ryan Stone Stories

- The Drone Factory
- The Dragon Boat Conspiracy
- Point of No Return
- The Obedience Keepers

www.amazon.com/author/benreinhart

HIGH TIDE AT GREEN KEY

Made in the USA
Columbia, SC
13 November 2023